Against his best judgement, Jack MacLaren allows Judge Harald Beck to talk him into pinning on the star again — just for a week. MacLaren's charge: fetch Burleigh Simmons from the Chama jail and deliver him to Beck's gallows.

While MacLaren is on the trail with Simmons, Victorio, the feared and respected Apache leader, seals his fate when he breaks off futile peace talks with the Army and takes up the hatchet against the white man in one of the last big Apache Wars.

Just when MacLaren thought he'd found peace and prosperity in the New Mexico Territory, he's sucked into the vortex of the storm and finds himself up against outlaws, politicians, a kid hell-bent on revenge, and his old friend Victorio.

Jack MacLaren knows they'll all take a long ride through the corridors of Hell before Apache Sundown.

Apache Sundown
Fiction
Published by:
Fanjoy & Bell, Ltd.
P.O. Box 5035
Manchester, NH 03108-5035
(800) 984-9798

Cover Art: *End of the Trail,* Copyright © 1988, by Marianne
Caroselli. Marianne Caroselli has been dedicated to painting and
sculpting for over twenty years. Many of her paintings have been
published as greeting cards, posters, and on calendars. She pres-
ently has twenty-five different bronzes available. Her work is
represented at nine galleries in New Mexico, Texas, Arizona, and
Colorado. For information, address Marianne Caroselli, 8511
Alydar Circle, Fair Oaks Ranch, TX 78015, Phone & FAX:
(210) 981-4544.

ISBN: 0-9652112-0-7

Printed in the United States of America

Apache Sundown

Ed Hewson

Fanjoy & Bell, Ltd.
P.O. Box 5035
Manchester, NH 03108-5035

For

Diana

The center of my universe.

PROLOG

In early April of 1879, Apache Chieftains Victorio and Loco, made camp on the edge of the compound at Fort Sumner in the New Mexico Territory. They were there with a hundred of their Mimbres Apache warriors to attend peace talks.

Victorio had been reluctant to meet with the white men. He'd lived through countless broken promises. But Loco had resigned himself to the notion that fighting the onslaught of white settlers and the U.S. Army was a futile enterprise which would lead to the destruction of his people. After days of argument, Loco had convinced Victorio to go to Fort Sumner to talk with the men from Washington.

Fourteen years had passed since the surrender at Appomattox and President Hayes was suffering through a stormy term in office as he struggled to restore the South to its proper place in the Republic. In recent months, the Eastern papers which were hostile to Hayes had fanned the isolated brush fires in the New Mexico Territory into a major political conflagration. The untamed territories had all the elements to fuel the fires of yellow journalism. Outlaw gangs operated freely. Ranchers fought bloody territorial wars. Apaches frequently bolted the reservations and killed white settlers. While any story of trouble in the territories could stir up folks back East, nothing got more play in the papers than a good bloody story about a band of Apache raiders raping and killing helpless white women.

On the first day of talks with Joseph A. Seth of the Bureau of Indian Affairs, and Colonel Hans Opitz of the U.S. Army, Victorio was overwhelmed with an utter sense of hopelessness when Seth opened the first meeting with a proposal which was essentially a list of handouts to be distributed at the Apache Reservation at San Carlos in the Arizona Territory.

"We are here to talk of a few more bags of flour crawling with

1

bugs!" Victorio shot back at Seth. "More worn out Army blankets and bad meat! More trinkets to be given at San Carlos, a place where evil spirits would not live!"

Loco raised his hand and, with a telling glance, suggested that Victorio calm down.

It was at that very instant that Victorio understood his fate. A certain calm fell over the Mimbres Chieftain. He said nothing for the rest of the session. Nonetheless he locked eyes with Colonel Opitz on several occasions. They were not friendly exchanges.

That evening, Victorio confronted Loco. "I will hear no more talk from the white man. I will leave at sunrise."

Loco saw into Victorio's heart. He knew his old friend would entertain no further argument.

It was a still, gray dawn when Victorio began to break camp. Awakened by a sentry, Colonel Opitz appeared in minutes. He pleaded with Victorio to stay for one more day of talks. Victorio refused. "Talk to Loco. He will hear your words," Victorio grunted at Opitz.

Opitz insisted but Victorio quietly tended to his horse, appearing to hear nothing Opitz said.

Shortly after Opitz stomped off, a company of buffalo soldiers appeared just beyond the perimeter of the Apache camp. In minutes they had established a circle of sentries.

The message was clear. The talks would continue, or else.

Victorio slipped into a silent rage. He knew what he had to do. Years earlier he had sworn an oath that he would never allow himself to suffer the same fate as his mentor and friend, the great Apache Chief, Mangas Coloradas. Under a flag of truce, Mangas Coloradas had suffered a humiliating death at the hands of the white soldiers. Nonetheless, Victorio's rage hadn't impaired his wisdom. He told his followers to restore the camp. They would stay.

Victorio sat through another day of talks. Setting the stage for his breakout, he appeared interested and even engaged in the give-and-take of the meetings.

Late that evening, he called together his people and gave them the option of staying with Loco to pursue peace or leaving with him before sunrise. Nana at his side, old Victorio spared no words in explaining what the escape would mean. He warned that the buffalo soldiers might not let them leave without a fight. "A fight tomorrow means war with the white man," Victorio insisted. "This time it will be a fight to the death."

Thirty eight of his best warriors quickly agreed to go, including a

2

group loyal to the bloodthirsty Ciervo Blanco. Nana, a fierce warrior in his own right, had a group of sixteen followers who didn't hesitate. And a handful of loners like the infamous, blue-eyed halfbreed, Cain, agreed to join in the breakout.

At sunrise the following day, a sentry riding the perimeter of Fort Sumner found the bodies of the dead buffalo soldiers who had been standing watch. Victorio and thirty-eight of his men had vanished.

Colonel Opitz had his hands full readying a patrol to hunt down Victorio while trying to protect the remaining Apaches from his own angry men. There was talk among the soldiers of slaughtering Loco and his followers.

By the end of the week, the Army hadn't even caught a glimpse of Victorio's dust, but it wasn't for the lack of a trail to follow. The band of renegades had left a trail of bodies halfway across the Territory.

The territorial papers were reporting record-breaking sales. They'd dubbed the bloody conflict, "The Victorio War."

For the next year, the battle would capture the collective attention of the nation and forever alter the lives of all those who got caught in the maelstrom of the last big Apache war.

1

Jack MacLaren stared across his campfire at Burleigh Simmons. Simmons ate his hardtack and jerked beef like a wolf tearing at the gut of a fresh-killed faun. MacLaren had dealt with some foul characters in his day, but he figured Simmons barely qualified as human.

MacLaren and his prisoner had made camp on the Purgatoire River northeast of the junction of Santa Fe Trail and the river. With no moon, the clear April sky was a mass of starlight. The temperature was falling rapidly and MacLaren wondered once again how he'd ever got talked into leaving his ranch to spend time on the trail with trash like Simmons.

"How about some more coffee, MacLaren?" Simmons asked, his squeaky voice almost comical in light of his large frame, mean eyes, and his reputation as a killer.

MacLaren got up and snatched the pot off the flat rock at the edge of the fire. "Hardly seems right wasting good coffee on a dead man," he said as he poured the steamy liquid into the cup held up by Simmons' manacled hands.

"They ain't stretched my neck yet, MacLaren. And we got a ways to go before Santa Fe," Simmons said. "And I got friends."

MacLaren shrugged. "I doubt you've ever had a friend, Simmons. Shut up and enjoy the stars. You won't be able to see them where you are going."

Simmons squeaked out one of his fiendish laughs and rocked back on his saddle and bedroll.

MacLaren poured more coffee, sat down on his oil cloth and once again put the soles of his boots to the fire. Judge Beck had warned him that Simmons had a small band of followers, each as deranged and vicious as Simmons, all unreconstructed Rebs who'd taken to a life of thieving and killing. The war had been over for fourteen years. But for thousands like Simmons the war wouldn't be over until the Devil fetched their souls for eternity. That was especially true for many of those like Simmons who'd ridden with the likes of Quantrill and Bloody Bill Anderson.

MacLaren understood how boys weaned on blood and Yankee reconstruction could ride the trail they'd chosen after the Civil War. He had often wondered what would have happened to him if he'd stuck out the war. The answer was always the same. He figured he'd have taken a fatal ball sooner or later. He often wished he knew who'd fired the pistol that had saved him from that certain death. He'd shake that Yankee's hand. Every day since the moment that slug had parted his hair had been a day worth living.

After having survived some of the bloodiest fighting of the war in Colonel George S. Patton's 23rd Virginia Battalion, Sergeant Jack MacLaren's war had ended at New Market in May of 1864. As Patton's infantry moved toward Smith's Creek, General Stahel's Yankee cavalry charged. The next thing MacLaren knew he was laid up in the Booker farm house on the north side of Lacey Springs. The woman who'd nursed him back to health said he'd wandered in with a blank mind and a scabbed-over furrow across the right side of his head. Though it had taken several years, MacLaren had since pieced together all but two weeks of that period of his life.

He'd stayed with Mrs. Mary Louise Booker and her two daughters for five months while he had regained his strength and most of his senses. Those five months had been some of the best days of his life. Even though Mary Louise had given up her man and two son's to the war, she'd never looked back. It was a rare day that went by without her crossing his mind. The war, once so important to him, had seemed like nonsense after his five months with Mary Louise. When he'd healed up, he'd simply headed west, convinced that he'd given enough blood to Jeff Davis and the rest of the politicians.

Simmons squeaky voice shattered the evening air. "Get some more wood on that fire MacLaren. I'm cold."

MacLaren didn't budge until he finished his coffee. Then he stoked the fire with the rest of the wood he'd gathered earlier in the evening.

"Off your arse, Simmons."

"Come on MacLaren you ain't gonna chain me up to a goddamn tree are you? Man can't sleep like that."

MacLaren snatched up his stubby shotgun, got the leg irons out of his saddle bags, and walked to the small tree he'd picked out when they'd made camp.

Simmons rolled over and got to his knees, all the time wondering how he might make a play for MacLaren's shotgun. He figured that MacLaren couldn't stay alert forever. He planned to strike the instant MacLaren let down his guard. Ever since they'd left the Chama jail, he'd been imagining the pleasure he'd take watching the life go out of Jack MacLaren's eyes.

MacLaren knew he was dealing with a cornered mountain lion. "Look cross-eyed at my twelve gauge and I'll use it to cut you in half, Simmons. Make my life easier if I took your head back to Judge Beck in a feed sack and left the rest for the buzzards."

Simmons sat down, pulled his boots off, and scooted up, putting the four inch tree trunk between his legs. He wasn't about to face MacLaren head on. MacLaren had a reputation in the New Mexico Territory. Folks said he was a fair man who was slow to anger. But they said that a provoked Jack MacLaren would just as soon shoot a man as stomp a bug. And Simmons knew that MacLaren's stubby twelve gauge would put a man down in a hurry.

MacLaren knelt, set the cocked shotgun on the ground with the twin bores pointed right at Simmons' crotch, and locked the irons on his prisoner's ankles.

"MacLaren, how the hell do you expect a man to sleep humped up on this tree?"

"It isn't your sleep I'm worried about," MacLaren said as he grabbed his shotgun, stood up, and backed away.

Simmons smiled. His pitted, brown teeth, deep eye sockets, and rat's nest beard were illuminated by the fire in a way that made him look precisely like the diabolical fiend he was.

MacLaren looked directly into Simmons' eyes. The sight once again made him wonder why he ever agreed to put on the U.S. Marshal's badge again, if only for a week. Then he seriously contemplated shooting Simmons on the spot. The trip to Santa Fe just for a public hanging served no purpose. It was a lot of trouble for everyone involved, Simmons included. He could put Simmons down with less upset than he'd have putting down an old hound.

Simmons was no fool. He read MacLaren's eyes. His smile vanished and he broke eye contact with the lawman.

MacLaren backed off another pace and kicked Simmons' bed roll toward his prisoner. He cursed under his breath as he lowered the external hammers on his shotgun and leaned the piece against his saddle, which he'd carefully positioned at the head of his oil cloth.

He was still grumbling to himself as he poured more coffee, and then settled back against his saddle to gnaw on a piece of jerked beef. Letting his friend, Harald Beck, talk him into putting on the badge had been a gross violation of his first rule for leading an uncomplicated life. "Mind your own damn business!" was the creed he'd come to live by in recent years. His idea of a friend was someone who never backed you into a corner.

But his ideas on most everything didn't often fit in the standard human puzzle.

That his friend Harald Beck had his hands full in the spring of 1879 was none of his bother. Beck's desire to do good held no attraction for MacLaren.

Beck, a lawyer and rancher, was one of the first men sought out by the newly appointed territorial governor, General Lew Wallace, formerly of Indiana. At age twenty-five, Beck had left his father's prestigious Philadelphia law firm and settled in Santa Fe in 1850. Beck had a reputation as a hard but honest man. He'd carved his ranch out of the open land east of Santa Fe while remaining at peace with the Indians. All the while he built a reputation as one of the best lawyers in the territory.

General Wallace had asked Beck to take the federal bench and restore order and justice to the territory. The new governor believed in a vengeful God. He wanted the killers, cattle rustlers, and horse thieves out of the territory or on the gallows.

Beck at once had asked his trusted friend and fellow rancher, Jack MacLaren, to wear the badge again. MacLaren had refused the appointment. And he'd begged off several other requests that he put on the gold star for short-term assignments. Finally invoking their friendship, by reminding MacLaren of several favors he'd rendered in the past, and claiming that his back was against the wall, Beck had convinced MacLaren to take on the job of bringing Burleigh Simmons to the hangman.

MacLaren had been cursing himself ever since he'd caved in to Beck.

As he watched the fire come to life, MacLaren decided his accounts with Beck were settled after he delivered Simmons to the hangman.

With the moisture baked out of the new wood, the fire warmed MacLaren's body. The flames dancing on a bed of hot coals, the soft noises of the horses, and the clear sky provided a perfect evening, flawed only by the presence of Burleigh Simmons.

"Jesus, MacLaren. You got another blanket. I'm likely to freeze to death."

"Go right ahead, Simmons. You'll save Governor Wallace the five dollar hangman's fee."

Forgetting the look on MacLaren's face only minutes earlier, Simmons lost his temper. "Goddamn you, MacLaren! When I get out of this, I'm going to cut you apart and take a day to do it!"

2

As the darkness turned gray, Jack MacLaren worked at a steady pace, brushing and then saddling his sixteen hand bay gelding. MacLaren was a fastidious man. He held to the proposition that a sloppy life leads to a sloppy mind and a flawed character.

Simmons slept soundly in spite of the tree between his legs.

When he finally had his horse tacked and his gear tied up and secured to his saddle, MacLaren poured another cup of coffee and walked over to his prisoner. He paused for a minute, looking down on the killer. In recent years he'd become increasingly baffled by the utter stupidity, greed, brutality, and downright dishonesty he'd encountered in so many men. Mostly, he shook it off to growing older. And he figured that the war hadn't helped matters much. Reconstruction had embittered the South. The raw, corrupt government power which had been sucked into the vacuum created by the utter devastation of the South was something most men couldn't accept. A part of MacLaren understood the subhuman at his feet. Though he couldn't imagine men like Simmons who'd kill a woman for the sheer pleasure of it. A raw spot in his soul understood how a man could step over the line, how a man could snap and discard all the conventions of his culture. He was a well read man and he'd often pondered the fragile line between right and wrong.

MacLaren took a slug of coffee with his left hand as he thumbed back both hammers on his shotgun.

"Get up Simmons," MacLaren said as he tapped Simmons arm with the toe of his boot.

As Simmons stirred, MacLaren tossed the stale contents of his cup, walked to the smoking remains of the fire and doused it with the dregs of the pot. After he'd secured the small pot and his cup in his plain, cowhide saddlebag, he walked back to Simmons and unlocked his leg irons, reminding himself to be careful. He'd had only a few hours sleep since he'd pulled Simmons from the Chama jail.

He reminded himself that one long day on the train and another in the saddle and he'd be rid of Burleigh Simmons. He was counting on everything going right. He had no idea that he was headed into events that would turn the coming year upside down.

Simmons scooted back from the tree and pulled on his boots. "MacLaren ain't you got breakfast ready yet?"

"We're moving out in five minutes, Simmons," MacLaren said, his stubby twelve gauge trained on his prisoner's gut. "We've got a train to catch and you've got a date with the hangman."

After two hours in the saddle, they were in the Trinidad Station waiting for the ten o'clock Denver & Rio Grande. In the past year the railroad had laid track all the way to Las Vegas, New Mexico, a thriving town just thirty-five miles east of Santa Fe. But politics had the railroad stalled in Las Vegas. The Denver & Rio Grande wanted to bypass Santa Fe and take a straight line to Albuquerque, a move that made business sense. The politicians wanted the rails to go west to Santa Fe, the territorial capital. However the rest of it worked out, the rails to Las Vegas had been a boon to MacLaren since he'd sold a right-of-way through his six thousand acre ranch for cash and a ten year guarantee on discounted freight rates. The days of the cattle drive to Denver were over for Jack MacLaren and he wasn't going to miss it. He was already planning to expand his other enterprises in Las Vegas, and he'd had it in mind to start a cattleman's bank.

The train was on time. MacLaren kept one eye on the men coaxing his horse into the stock car and the other on Simmons. Even though his hands were chained and his feet manacled to the leg of one of the heavy oak benches on the platform, MacLaren could read Simmons' mind. He knew Simmons, although calm on the outside, was boiling with anger, possessed with the idea of seeing him dead.

MacLaren had arranged to travel in the express car, reminding the stationmaster that he wouldn't hesitate to kill Simmons and he didn't want any civilians blooded in the process.

When the "Alamosa No.22," a new, brightly painted Baldwin 2-8-0, pulled out of the station an 10:35, MacLaren's package was settled among the other baggage in the express car, his feet chained to an iron hold-down ring recessed in the floor. Though the rings were not designed to hold down human cargo, they met MacLaren's needs perfectly. Like the engine, the car was new and the smell of fresh varnish permeated the air. A quarter mile out of the Trinidad station, the Baldwin hit the steady incline that would not cease until it crested the seventy-eight hundred foot crease at Raton Pass.

MacLaren, a man with a bottomless curiosity, had only ridden the new line once to Denver and back, so he was intrigued by the trip, and he was especially interested in the doings of the on-board express agent, who quickly sorted packages and mail and attended to mountains of paperwork.

Oddly, paperwork always reminded him of his father. MacLaren's family and been in the lumber business before the war took everything they had, including the lives of his father, and two older brothers. Though his mother survived the war, she'd never put her life back together and she'd died before her time in 1871. His earliest memories were of the sawmill, the giant silver blade slicing effortlessly through logs. And he always remembered his father shuffling papers at his giant oak roll-top desk. Even though they were fond memories, and MacLaren was one of the more successful businessmen in the Territory, he couldn't bring himself to do office work. He hated it. He hired people to do it. All of it. He could sink fence posts all day in the hot sun, but five minutes of paper shuffling was five minutes too much.

By the time he was ten, he was working in the mill, and already showing an aptitude for mechanical things, an aptitude still only second to his way with horses. He tried to strike up a conversation with the agent, hoping to learn more about the new Baldwin locomotive but the agent didn't know a steam engine from a wagon wheel.

"God damnit!" Simmons squeaked all of a sudden. "Get me something to eat. You ain't got the right to starve a man."

MacLaren turned and looked at his prisoner, his temper flaring. If eyes had the power to kill, Simmons would be dead. "You aren't a man, Simmons. You're vermin."

The agent took a biscuit from a wrinkled paper sack on his desk and handed it to Simmons. "What did he do?" the agent asked MacLaren.

"Nothing out of the ordinary for his kind. He and four of his friends took liberties with a family of tin pans down near Hurley, folks who came West to make a fortune panning gold."

"Damned if they didn't have some dust," Simmons said, his mouth full of biscuit. "Wasn't but a couple of ounces. Enough for a night of wore out whores and cheap whiskey."

"A thief?" the agent asked MacLaren.

"That, and rape and murder. After they forced the tin pans to give up their dust, they tied up the man and his boy and made them watch as they raped the woman and the girl for several hours. Hurley sheriff said they carved on the woman and her fourteen-year-old daughter for some time. Sheriff said they went out real slow. Guess they finally felt sorry for the men. They just gave them each a .45 caliber slug in the forehead, after they made them watch the show of course."

The agent backed toward his desk and took a sudden interest in his mail sorting and invoices.

MacLaren looked over at Simmons.

"That little girl was some good, MacLaren. I think she liked it. And her Ma weren't so bad neither," Simmons said.

Another moment of rage flushed through MacLaren's body and then passed as quickly as it came. "Simmons. Shut your mouth or I'll tie you by your feet and drag you to Las Vegas behind this train."

Simmons shrugged and stuffed the remainder of his biscuit in his grotesque face.

His friend Harald Beck had said, "Bring Simmons to justice!" At that moment MacLaren was thinking that hanging Simmons wouldn't come close to balancing the scales of justice. He figured that the Apaches couldn't even come up with something that could balance the books on Burleigh Simmons.

It was almost midnight by the time the train pulled into Las Vegas Station. Although it was only a hundred and twenty miles, frequent stops for passengers, freight, livestock, water and wood brought the average speed to ten miles an hour.

At the previous stop, MacLaren had wired the new Deputy U.S. Marshal in Las Vegas, requesting that he meet the train. He was going to lock Simmons in the local jail, and, after a long bath and a few fingers of good Kentucky bourbon, spend the night in his private suite in his William Bell Hotel.

Harley Adair was waiting on the platform when the train ground to a stop. MacLaren hauled Simmons from the express car and approached the young man with the shiny star on his leather vest.

"You Adair?" MacLaren asked.

"Yes sir," Adair said directly.

"Hang on to this trash," he said as he pushed Simmons toward the Marshal and stomped off to tend to the horses.

In a quick minute MacLaren had issued chain of orders to everyone from the stable boy to the railroad agent.

"Let's go," was all MacLaren said as he approached and passed Simmons and Adair without a pause.

MacLaren realized Adair was new like everybody else in the Wallace administration. And since MacLaren had never met the young man, he went to the jail with the deputy and made sure Simmons was sealed behind bars before he let down his guard.

"You men listen up," MacLaren said to the guard and two jail-house idlers. "No one opens this cell for any reason. Not even fire. Let the son-of-a-bitch burn to death. You all got that? Pass his chow through the bars and let him shit in his bucket."

With that, Simmons went berserk, rattling his cell door and shouting a string of oaths.

MacLaren turned on his heel and walked out, leaving the young federal deputy a dozen paces behind.

"Hold up Mister MacLaren," the deputy said catching up.

MacLaren kept walking in a straight line to his hotel, but he turned his head and said, "Call me Jack."

"I've got a message from Judge Beck."

"What's he want now?" MacLaren grunted.

"Said to tell you that Victorio and three dozen of his warriors busted out of Fort Sumner earlier today. Killed six buffalo soldiers on the way out." MacLaren stopped dead in his tracks and turned to face Adair.

"That's all the Judge said, Harley?"

"Except he said you and Victorio are friends. Judge Beck said the Chief is headed west and likely to leave a bloody trail behind."

3

MacLaren stopped for a drink in the gambling parlor and saloon which took up half of the first floor of his hotel. Like the hotel, the saloon was plain but neatly appointed and clean.

Billy Wilcomb, part owner and manager of the hotel was hustling behind the busy bar, trying to keep glasses full.

"Jack," Wilcomb said as MacLaren approached the massive oak bar which covered most of one wall. "Glad to see you back. Word has it Simmons' gang's out looking for him and you both. Folks have been worried."

"I know a few folks in town who must be rooting for Simmons."

"No doubt, Jack."

"The usual, Billy. I need to wash away some dust and get the stink of Simmons out of my throat."

Wilcomb poured MacLaren's favorite bourbon into a short glass. "I expect you want to know what I've heard about Victorio," he said as he pushed the full glass toward MacLaren.

Maclaren took a gulp of bourbon and nodded.

Considering the feelings of most people when it came to Apaches, and considering MacLaren's reputation as a man that didn't hold with the way the government had treated the Indians, no one ever approached MacLaren on the subject of his friendship with Victorio and his son Nana. Billy Wilcomb was indifferent to the fate of the Apaches. But he saw through MacLaren's leathery exterior and understood his friendship with Victorio. Though it did worry him. It was Jack MacLaren's loyalty to the people he called friends that often got him in hot water.

"Nothing much yet, Jack. You knew they had them corralled up outside Fort Sumner for peace talks. Word has it they've been through a rough winter at San Carlos. They figure the agent at San Carlos has been cheating them."

"That bastard's been shortin' the Chief and his people ever since he got there. He ought to be strung up next to Simmons."

"Not likely," Wilcomb said. "Those Bureau types are all connected in Washington. And nobody much cares how the Apache is treated."

MacLaren looked up from his glass, annoyed with Wilcomb's tone.

"Hey, Jack, don't put that look on me, I'm just talkin' facts," Wilcomb shot back.

"How many warriors left with him?" MacLaren asked directly.

"Sounds like thirty or forty," Wilcomb answered. "His best men, no doubt."

MacLaren just shook his head. Victorio and forty good Apache warriors could raise enough hell to turn the territory upside down, and in the end, seal their own fates.

"Any word on where they're headed?" MacLaren asked Wilcomb.

"It looks like they're headed north west, up the Pecos River. Can't tell if it's just rumor, but a teamster who just came through with a load from Fort Sumner said a dozen settlers have already met their maker."

MacLaren slid his glass across the bar for a refill. "If Victorio's set on fighting one last war, they'll be more than a few making an early trip to Hell."

Billy Wilcomb filled the glass and hustled off to pump beer for a pair of range hands who'd gone dry.

The bourbon began to relax MacLaren and remind him how tired he was. He'd only closed his eyes on Simmons a couple of times. But the news about his friend Victorio saddened him. He knew that this would be the Chief's last war. He doubted that he'd ever see him again. But he also understood. He respected Victorio. MacLaren was one of those rare men who sincerely believed that there were things more important than life itself. Victorio had been on reservations before, and sooner or later he always broke out. The U.S. Army had never captured him. Each time Victorio had ceased hostilities voluntarily and signed his mark on a peace treaty, only to have it broken by the white man. MacLaren knew that this time, the Chief and his son, Nana, would be hunted down and killed. He knew Victorio understood that it would be a fight to the death. America was moving West, and there was no room for the Apache in the new scheme of things.

"Another, Jack?" Wilcomb asked.

"No thanks, Billy. I need a hot bath and some sleep. I still have to get Simmons to Santa Fe."

"What ever possessed you to pin the badge on again, Jack? Never figured you would sit in on that game again, even for a week."

"No more surprised than me, Billy. I've been kicking myself in the ass ever since Beck pulled me into the corner with his little talk about duty, honor, and friendship. Guess he figures that he and Governor Wallace can still save the world. Mark my word, Beck gets his badge back when I shut the cell door on Simmons in Santa Fe."

"Good, I've got a few things to talk over with you. Some ideas on how we might improve operations here."

"Not now, Billy. Let me get Simmons to Santa Fe and then we'll talk. I know I've been neglecting business here. But I need some sleep. I want to be on the trail again before the sun's up," MacLaren said as he turned and headed for the stairs.

"Mary Beth stopped by earlier, wondering if you'd arrived yet. You going to stop over and see her?"

"When I get back from Santa Fe," he said over his shoulder.

MacLaren climbed the wide, heavy timber stairs to his suite on the second floor. In minutes he settled into a hot bath. He wondered as he had many times about the odd course his life had taken. Victorio and his ancestors had roamed these lands for thousands of years. In just a few years the white man had overrun the territory, wiped out most of the Indians and corralled the rest on nasty land where they were cheated out of their federal rations, given pox-infected blankets, and robbed of their last bit of dignity, all in the name of economic progress, Christianity, and the theory of manifest destiny. While, MacLaren felt the injustice of it all, he was one of the chief benefactors of the taming and settling of the New Mexico Territory. His ranch and his business enterprises in Las Vegas were making money so fast it was piling up in his bank faster than he could reinvest it.

At one moment he could be euphoric about the whole thing. After working twelve hours straight on a new section of fencing on his ranch, he could stand back and marvel at life and feel satisfied that it meant something. At other times he could be overcome by the utter stupidity of man and the sheer hopelessness of life. He knew time would whisk away a new section of fence or a wooden hotel just as surely as it would his very life.

16

4

The young Adair had his horse tacked up when MacLaren arrived at the livery at five the next morning. He insisted on making the trip to Santa Fe. The Deputy U.S. Marshal claimed he was under orders from Judge Beck.

MacLaren's pride was slightly bruised over the idea that Beck figured he needed help from the young man, but he also figured a little companionship and an extra hand wouldn't hurt. During his walk to the livery, MacLaren decided to avoid the main road to Santa Fe by taking the northern route through Mineral Hill and Vallecitos. It would add another day to the forty mile ride, but it would be safer.

"I don't mind you coming along, Harley. But I want you to understand what you're dealing with here."

Adair nodded.

"How old are you?" MacLaren asked.

"Twenty-four," Adair answered proudly.

"Ever killed a man?" MacLaren asked as he cross-tied his gelding in the isle of the stable.

"No sir."

"Well, I want you to kill Simmons if he even looks at us the wrong way," MacLaren said, his piercing blue eyes fixed on Adair. "The Territory has already passed sentence on him. The hangman gets five dollars for his knowhow with the rope and scaffold. Those cartridges in your Colt sell for three cents each. You'd be doing Governor Wallace a favor and saving him four dollars and change. Simmons, by conservative count, has killed two dozen people, women and children included, not to mention the folks he slaughtered with Quantrill and Bill Anderson."

"Yes sir," Adair said, confident he could do whatever was needed.

MacLaren liked what he saw in the young man's long, angular face and clear, hazel eyes. He looked like a man who could handle himself. But that didn't make him rest any easier. Playing deputy marshal in the New Mexico Territory in the spring of 1879 was a dangerous business.

MacLaren laid out procedures for watching Simmons as he had saddled his sixteen hand bay gelding with his elegantly plain, well oiled and polished gear. There was nothing fancy about MacLaren in his dress, his talk, his business operations, or his sprawling log ranch house. Nonetheless everything about him, was striking in its simplicity and utility.

"One more time, Harley, before we get to the jailhouse," MacLaren said. "Don't hesitate to shoot Simmons if it comes to that. I'll back you all the way. I nearly shot him myself on the trail from Chama. Mark my word. If he gets the drop on you he'll kill you certain."

* * * *

There was only a faint orange light on the eastern plain as MacLaren, Adair, and Simmons mounted up in front of the Las Vegas jail.

The morning passed easily as the trio moved toward Santa Fe under the clear Spring sky. Although it was not the main trail, the path through the virgin woods was worn and wide enough for wagon passage. For the most part, Simmons remained quiet. When he did talk his squeaky voice was as unsettling as a sidewinder on your bed-roll.

The noon sun, unobstructed by a single cloud, warmed the earth rapidly and the horses soon broke into a mild sweat. MacLaren began looking for a grassy clearing to break for an hour to graze and rest the horses and fix grub.

It wasn't long before they broke into a clearing. Adair was in the lead, with MacLaren trailing behind Simmons. A hundred yards across the grassy strip on the edge of a stand of cottonwood trees, they saw a camp. There was a ten-foot-square canvas lean-to, a wagon, and smoke drifting from a camp fire.

"Looks like some folks have the same idea we have," Adair said, turning in his saddle. "May as well join them."

"Hold up, Harley," MacLaren said. "I don't like the look of it."

The deputy threw MacLaren a puzzled look.

18

"You keep your Colt trained on Simmons' left eye. I'm going to circle the edge of the woods and approach from the other side."

Adair still looked perplexed.

"What do you see, boy," MacLaren said, noticing Adair's bewilderment.

"Wagon. Tent. Fire."

"What don't you see?" MacLaren asked as he nudged his horse off the trail at a slow trot.

Adair suddenly understood. No horses. No people. It appeared to be an empty camp and nothing else.

In five minutes, MacLaren appeared at the other side of the clearing. "Come on in," MacLaren shouted.

Adair wasn't prepared for what he saw as he approached. There were bodies everywhere. A man. A woman. Two girls and a boy. All laying in their own blood.

"Looks like my boys have been here," Simmons said as he rocked back in his saddle and roared with mock laughter.

MacLaren snatched his shotgun from its sheath, thumbed back both hammers, and pointed the twin tubes at the killer. "Keep talking, Simmons."

Simmons knew he was a dead man if he even exhaled loudly.

"Chain him to that wagon wheel," MacLaren said to Adair, pointing the shotgun toward the large rear wheel of the decrepit freight wagon which had been converted to a make-shift home on wheels. "I'm going to have a look around. There's still embers in that fire. I'd guess the Apaches have been gone for a couple of hours. But I want to make sure."

MacLaren reined his horse around and walked into the woods, his short twelve gauge out of its sheath and cradled in his lap.

Adair cautiously chained Simmons to the wheel and then walked from body to body, dazed by what he saw, suddenly aware of the smell of death. The men and women had been shot and mutilated and the flies were already feeding at the gaping wounds and open eyes.

MacLaren rode back into camp, dismounted and slid his shotgun back into its scabbard. "Apaches. My guess is twenty warriors. The tracks meet up with another group of about ten ponies further down the road."

Suddenly they heard a sound to their left. Before MacLaren could turn, Adair's Colt had cleared leather and he was set in a crouch, his revolver trained toward the sound.

One of the bodies was moving, a boot pushed rhythmically on the soft earth.

5

Momentarily taken aback by Adair's prowess with his Colt, MacLaren turned toward the deputy, but his surprised look did not distract Adair who was still focused on the moving body.

The foot pushed against the ground another time and stopped. Adair relaxed his stance, holstered his revolver, and approached the boy who was face down in the grass, one arm outstretched, the other beneath his body. His blue calico shirt was blood-soaked. His long blond hair was matted with dark dried blood.

MacLaren moved quickly to the boy and felt for a pulse on the side of his neck. He couldn't feel a pulse, but he knew the boy wasn't dead. His skin was still pliable, and the muscles in his neck were soft. MacLaren had seen enough dead men to know one at a glance.

"See if you can find a blanket in the wagon, Harley," MacLaren said as he pulled his knife from its sheath and slit the kid's shirt from his belt to his collar.

Once he'd laid open the shirt, he saw the wound. A slug had caught the kid in the side, followed his ribs just under the skin, and ripped a three inch exit wound in his back. It looked bad, but it wasn't a fatal wound.

"Spread it next to him," MacLaren commanded as Adair approached with a red plaid blanket. "I want to turn him over."

Adair quickly unfurled the blanket and helped MacLaren roll the boy face up.

"Jesus Christ," Adair wheezed when he saw the wound in the kid's head. He had a five inch crease on the left side of his head which laid his scalp wide open. There wasn't a hole in the boy's skull, just pealed skin and hair all stuck up with dried blood. His eyes were closed and the rest of his face looked peaceful. The boy's hand gripped a new .450 Boxer Colt single action Army Model revolver.

20

MacLaren carefully put his finger between the cocked hammer and the frame and removed the Colt from the boy's hand. He bent over and put his ear to the boy's mouth. "He's bad, but his breathing is steady. Harley, stoke that fire and get some fresh water from the creek." MacLaren drew his knife and cut another hole in his shirt looking for the beginning of the wound on his side.

While Adair was busy with the fire and water, MacLaren began gathering what he needed from the things strewn about the camp site by the Apaches.

"Guess this will mess up our little ride to Santa Fe," Simmons said, his grating nasal voice more irritating than ever.

MacLaren made like he didn't hear the killer as he began to tear a blue cotton dress into squares. But his six foot frame was hot with frustration and rage. He was again brimming with the disgust he felt over bending to Beck's pressuring him into wearing the badge again. In the last couple of years, MacLaren had, for the first time in his life, accepted things the way they were and had thoroughly convinced himself that life was what it was and nothing more. He no longer found solace in what might be. His visions of the future had given way to the present. Except for the moment, life was essentially meaningless. Politics, religious crusading, the anti-saloon league, and a hundred other causes were, in view of human nature, laughable. In the grand scheme of things, another five hundred feet of fence on the edge of his grasslands was worth more than any reverend's Sunday exhortations on the hereafter. He was standing in the middle of blood and gore, taunted and threatened by a subhuman killer, about to sew up a half-dead boy who was probably shot by his friend Victorio or one of his warriors.

MacLaren laid the bandages next to the boy and then retrieved a pouch of salt and a small sewing kit from his saddle bags. The sewing gear was something he always carried, owing to his penchant for order and neatness.

Within minutes, Adair had readied a small pot of hot water. MacLaren added salt, soaked the cloth squares, and applied them to the boys wounds, all of which had stopped bleeding.

"Harley," MacLaren said. We're going to be here for a while. Until the boy dies or gets better, one. Check his folks and the two girls. I'm sure they're dead, but check anyhow. I saw a shovel in the wagon. We've got to get these people buried before the sun works on them much longer. I'm going to have to sew this boy up after I clean the wounds. My guess, he won't make it. He's barely hanging on. But we've got to give it a try."

* * * *

The sun was deep in the western sky by the time Harley Adair had covered the fourth grave.

The boy, though still unconscious, was breathing steadily and his eyes still reacted to light when MacLaren pulled back the kid's eyelids. MacLaren had shaved back the kids blond hair with the razor sharp knife he always carried on his belt, and spent over an hour sewing fifteen single stitches in the crease in his scalp, followed by several stitches in the wounds on the boy's side.

MacLaren continued to soak the rags in hot salt water, frequently changing the compresses.

"Those folks are covered up," Adair said as he approached MacLaren.

MacLaren looked up at a ragged Adair standing above him in a sweat soaked, dirty shirt.

"Never seen anything like it," the deputy said as he looked down on the kid.

"You'll see worse if you keep that tin badge pinned on, son."

"Where did you learn that doctorin'?"

"The war. Hardly a man who came through it who can't doctor a saber wound, a bullet hole, or a busted bone."

"Ain't that for certain," Simmons said, more talking to himself than to the two lawmen.

"You said it was Apaches?" Adair asked, as he pushed his straight black hair out of his face. "How do you know? Couldn't it be Simmons men?"

"I just know. The tracks I followed into the woods. They're Apache ponies."

"Victorio?"

"Likely."

MacLaren saw the look on the deputy's face, a puzzled expression that was wondering what MacLaren saw in the Apache chief and his son Nana, savages who would wantonly slaughter people and mutilate women.

"It's war, Harley, war, Apache style. It's never pretty no matter how you dress it up," MacLaren said, attempting to answer the deputy's look.

Adair was silent as he looked down on the boy's peaceful face and stitched up skull. But the peace was broken when Simmons started squawking about dinner. Adair's temper suddenly flared. He walked

22

to Simmons, grabbed him by his collar and pulled until Simmons hands were straining against the manacles. "One more god damn word out of you, Simmons, I kick your ass so hard you'll be fartin' through your mouth for the rest of your short life!"

Simmons smiled, exposing his rotten teeth in Adair's face, the smile of the devil about to bring another soul into his realm. "You'd better keep a close watch, boy," Simmons whispered. "Or you're mine."

6

The cool evening air descended on the camp as the sun settled beyond the mountains. MacLaren added more wood to the fire and settled back on a crude wooden stool he'd found in the wagon. The injured boy lay still under the canvas lean-to.

In the last light, Adair was still cleaning up the camp site and piling the dead family's belongings in the wagon.

"Looks like a damn whirlwind went through here," Adair said as he stuffed a handful of women's garments into a wooden trunk.

MacLaren chuckled to himself as he watched Adair scurry around like a squirrel gathering acorns after the first hard frost. It was as if his cleaning up might somehow make everything right again.

Adair approached MacLaren with a worn family Bible. "Found this in the trunk," he said as he held the tattered book toward MacLaren.

MacLaren looked up at the young deputy, grunted, and took another sip of coffee.

"We forgot to say words over those folks, Jack."

"Think it'll do them any good, son?"

Adair seemed surprised by MacLaren's indifference. "It's natural to say something, isn't it? Doesn't seem right to lay people down without a few words from the Book."

"I don't see anyone stopping you," MacLaren snapped.

Adair's eyes grew wide in disbelief.

MacLaren groaned, got up, and walked toward the four mounds of dirt. "Come on, boy. Let's get it done before dark." At the graves, MacLaren snatched his dark brown, flat-brimmed Stetson off his head and looked off toward the mountains.

"Go on, Harley. Read your Bible," MacLaren said.

"I'm no preacher," Adair answered.

24

MacLaren let out a impatient sigh.

Adair opened the Bible at the page marked with a faded blue ribbon. "There's verses underlined here. Maybe they held special meaning for these folks."

"Maybe."

Adair began reading slowly, like a schoolboy reciting his lessons. "What does a man gain by all the toil at which he toils under the sun? A generation goes and a generation comes, but the earth remains forever. The sun rises and the sun goes down, and hastens to the place where it rises. The wind blows to the south, and goes round to the north; round and round goes the wind, and on its circuits the wind returns. All streams run to the sea, but the sea is not full; to the place where the streams flow, there they flow again. All things are full of weariness; a man cannot utter it; the eye is not satisfied with seeing, nor the ear filled with hearing. What has been is what will be, and what has been done will be done; and there is nothing new under the sun. And...."

"Amen," MacLaren interrupted as he thumped his hat back in place and headed back to the fire. Simmons had been out of his sight for several minutes and that made him uncomfortable.

"Rest in peace!" Adair said as he slapped the Bible closed, turned on his heel, and hurried after MacLaren.

* * * *

MacLaren and Adair sat quietly staring into the fire or looking at the boy for any signs that the kid was coming back to life. Lack of sleep and the events of the day had taken their toll on the two men. The fire burned on a large bed of red embers, radiating heat toward the lean-to. The black sky was alive with stars. "This would have been a good night to spend on my eastern range," MacLaren said. "Sit in front of a huge fire with my foreman, Joe Harper, and some of the boys. Dog tired after a twelve hour day. My dog at my side. Sippin' whiskey and telling lies."

"Sounds good," Adair said.

"It is good. Exact opposite of sitting here lookin' on that trash Simmons chained to a wagon. And that hurt kid," MacLaren added, pointing to the boy.

The orange light of the fire illuminated the injured boy's peaceful face. His only sign of life was his steady, shallow breathing.

MacLaren and Adair had moved the kid under the canvas shelter and laid him out near the fire. They'd covered him with blankets and cushioned his head with a feather pillow from the wagon. During his cleanup, Adair had found several things that obviously belonged to the boy and he had piled them next to the kid. The neat pile looked like a shrine at the boy's head. Though Adair couldn't imagine it belonging to the kid, he'd found the holster and belt for the Army Colt they'd taken from the boy's hand. He'd put the Colt back in its leather, wound the belt around the rig, and placed it with the rest of the things he'd piled next to the boy.

"What do you want to do tomorrow?" Adair asked MacLaren.

"I want you to ride on to Mineral Hill. Have someone there carry a message to Judge Beck explaining our situation. And then bring back help. A doctor if they have one. And we'll need a team of mules for the wagon."

"I don't like leaving you with Simmons," Adair said. "Those Apaches could still be around and Simmons friends are still on the lose."

"Victorio's making his way west to the Arizona territory, or maybe south to Old Mexico. I guarantee you he's not sticking around here. And I doubt Simmons' boys are going to risk their hides over trash like him. Probably drunk somewhere laying with six-bit whores."

"We take care of our own, MacLaren," Simmons said from his bed under the wagon. The tone of his voice was growing meaner by the hour. His hands were manacled, one on either side of one of the heavy oak rear wheels with the chain through the spokes. Likewise his feet were chained to the front wheel. His arms were stretched over his head since it was more than eight feet between the wagon axles. He was uncomfortable, sore, cold, and beginning to doubt that his outlaw friends were looking for him. And the thought of mounting a scaffolding in front of a jeering, half-drunk crowd, and falling through a trap door with a rope around his neck was beginning to unnerve him. His rage was rising to new heights. Every time he went to sleep, he had the same nightmare. He was watching himself dancing on air, as he soiled himself, his neck grotesquely stretched three feet long, the crowd overcome with laughter. The night before, in the Las Vegas jail, he had actually pissed his pants before awakening from his nightmare. Simmons focused all his fear and anger on his plans for MacLaren and Adair. For Burleigh Simmons, murder was better than poking the best whore in the territory, especially the kind of murder he was planning for the two lawmen.

MacLaren and Adair ignored Simmons frequent outbursts and set a plan for watching Simmons through the night.

"You remember what I told you at the livery this morning, Harley. I saw the way you handled that Colt earlier today. You know what you're doing with that hardware," he said pointing to Adair's side-arm. "But that doesn't always translate when it comes to pulling the trigger on a man. It's not the same as shooting whiskey bottles off a fence rail."

Adair nodded, and looked directly at MacLaren.

His eyes convinced MacLaren that the deputy would pull the trigger on Simmons if the need arose.

7

Adair had the last watch and he was glad to be awake. He'd gotten little sleep. Every time he'd dozed off, he'd have the same nightmare. The dead family arose from their graves. Stark naked, they walked aimlessly around the camp looking at and pointing to their gaping bloodless wounds, each seemingly oblivious to the others.

The young deputy couldn't cast off the images of the mutilated ghosts. The dreams were more vivid and unsettling than the real carnage he'd seen the day before. Harley Adair was young and a man of the world, but, like most young men, he'd been brought up to believe in an all-knowing, vengeful God, and a Devil with powers equal to those of God.

He was becoming increasingly restless as the gray sky in the east began to overtake the blackness, and restore his vision. And like any good Sunday school graduate, Harley knew the Devil always vanished at dawn.

Simmons appeared to be sleeping, MacLaren was snoring, and the wounded kid hadn't moved a muscle since they'd laid him out.

Adair got off the stool and threw more wood in the fire even though it didn't need any. As he began to settle back on the stool, he heard the horses fidgeting and moving awkwardly against the hobbles on their front feet. Bored with sitting, he decided to check the horses. Staked out thirty feet from the campsite, the horses were standing quietly. He walked around the three mounts, stopping at MacLaren's sixteen hand bay. He stroked the horse's warm shiny neck, admiring the gelding's big bone and near perfect conformation.

"You sure are a handsome boy, Gunn," Adair whispered as he ran his hand down the horse's neck, across his shoulder, and then down his front leg as he went down on one knee to inspect the leather hobble.

It was then that he heard the squeak of boot leather. He jumped up and began to turn, his hand going for the walnut grips on his Colt. But he turned into a rifle butt which caught him hard between the eyes. The blow didn't hurt. He just felt a jolt, and his vision closed in like he was looking through a stovepipe. His knees buckled. The world went black, and he pitched forward into the dew-soaked grass.

At the moment Adair had gone down, MacLaren spun out of his bed roll only to end up staring at the rusty, octagonal muzzle of a Winchester carbine.

"You jest holt still, mister. I'd sooner kill ya than poke your sister. Fact is, I would have kilt ya by now, 'ceptin I figured ole Burleigh'd be sore if I stolt the pleasure due him."

MacLaren knew the man meant it. Like Simmons, the short, fat creature under the filthy, ragged sombrero wasn't human.

Adair became vaguely aware of voices and being dragged feet first across wet grass.

"Git his pretty knife. Bailey," the fat man covering MacLaren said to one of the two outlaws who'd just dropped Adair's legs. Check him for a hideout, and find the keys to them chains he's got wrapped on Burleigh. And fetch me that shotgun," he added pointing MacLaren's stubby twelve gauge.

MacLaren's first reaction was resignation, he silently cursed Judge Beck and then accepted the fact that he was about to take a slow trip to hell. Still somewhat groggy from a deep sleep, he figured his streak of good luck had run out. Then suddenly, in a flash of visceral anger, those thoughts vanished as his heart began to pound, pumping survival juices through his system. MacLaren's instincts kicked in. His face got hot and his eyes automatically darted around the camp, assessing the situation. The one called Bailey fingered the manacle keys from the pocket in his leather vest, and then carefully slipped his knife from it's oiled and polished cowhide sheath. It wasn't in his nature to accept this predicament, even though the odds were long. He'd decided, he was going to take someone with him. Oddly, he thought again of Beck's speech about duty and honor and how he'd violated his rule about minding his own business. It was a good rule. He'd broken it, he thought to himself, and he was likely to pay for that transgression with his life. Then he smiled to himself, remembering how close he'd come to killing Simmons a couple of times in the preceding days. He was smiling because another of his carved-in-stone rules was to always allow his instincts to prevail over the conventional rules.

"You think this is funny, Marshal?" the fat man with the carbine said as he pressed the muzzle hard to MacLaren's forehead. Without taking his eyes off MacLaren, he took MacLaren's knife from the one called Bailey.

"Unlock Burleigh," the fat man under the sombrero said to Bailey.

MacLaren allowed the smile to pass slowly as he fixed his steel blue eyes directly on the eyes of his tormentor. MacLaren's look unnerved the fat outlaw, who briefly turned his eyes away to glance at Bailey as the outlaw struggled to remove Simmons' chains.

"Aaaahh," Adair moaned as the pain set in and he began to become aware of his predicament.

"Shut up," the third intruder said as he kicked Adair hard in the ribs. A rat-faced man with cratered cheeks and greasy, long, black hair protruding from a dirty bowler, this third intruder made Simmons look like well-groomed storekeep.

Adair grunted as the wind went out of his lungs and a spray of blood shot from his broken nose.

Simmons, who had been surprisingly quiet, was now free of his shackles.

"Stand him up and chain him to that wagon," Simmons said, pointing to Adair. "And don't be kickin' him and beatin' on him no more. I want these boys in awake condition so's they can watch themselves die." Simmons turned to the squat, fat man, who still had his carbine on MacLaren's forehead. "Where's the rest of the boys, Slim? How come there's only the three of you?"

"Dead, Burleigh. We all set camp and then me, Bailey, and T.J. went ahead lookin' for you. When we come back, Jake, Swan, Corky....the whole lot was kilt. Injuns done it. Chopped 'em to pieces too! Likely Chief Victorio and Nana. Word has it they've took up the hatchet again."

"It was Victorio who raided this camp," Simmons said. "That savage done the same here. That boy's head shot and the rest of his kin's gone to hell," Simmons said, pointing to the boy laid out under the canvas, and then to the four distant mounds of dirt which were now visible in the early morning light.

"Well, god damnit, Burleigh, lets get out of here!" Slim said, his Winchester still pressed to MacLaren's forehead. "We ain't got time to hang around here while you take your god damned pleasures and carve on these people."

"Yeah," the other two said in unison as they locked the manacle rings on Adair's wrists.

"Simmons snatched MacLaren's knife, blade first, out of Slim's hand. "I'll say what we got time for. I intend to settle up with these here law dogs. And it might take a while. You boys do like I said. Drag the deputy to the wagon and chain him to the wagon wheel."

MacLaren saw an opening as the fat one called Slim backed off with his Winchester. MacLaren rolled to his left. He was just about out of Slim's line of fire when Simmons lunged and came down on the top of his head with the heavy butt of his own knife. Stunned by the blow, the lawman fell back and went momentarily limp. Within seconds, a stabbing pain shot up his left arm. Something warm dripped on his face. The pain brought his eyes back in focus and he saw Simmons holding the end of a finger inches from his face.

"A piece at a time, MacLaren. That's how I'm gonna send you to Hell. A piece at a time," Simmons said, his squeaky voice ringing in MacLaren's ears like the wheel of a locomotive spinning on steel track. Then he tossed MacLaren's finger tip into the fire.

The other three outlaws giggled nervously like kids shooting bull frogs with a .22.

The pain in MacLaren's hand and arm and brought him to his senses, but he acted dazed. Although every muscle in his body was charged, he forced himself to appear limp and senseless.

Slim, the fat man, put the Winchester an inch from MacLaren's face. "Now git up," Slim said.

MacLaren, feigning dizziness, got up and staggered toward the wagon, urged forward by the muzzle of the Winchester which stabbed at his spine.

Simmons followed and then faced Adair.

Although, his head pounded with a thumping pain, Adair was acutely aware of his predicament.

"What did I tell you, boy?" Simmons asked, his nasal squeak almost comical. With that, he grabbed Adair's right ear and came down the side of the young deputy's head with MacLaren's razor sharp knife.

"Nahhhh," Adair grunted as he felt a tug and then warm blood flowing into his collar and down his chest.

Simmons held the ear in Adair's face and then flipped it over his shoulder. "I'm goin' to make you eat the next one, boy. But first me and your friend here's gonna have some fun while you watch and think about what your other ear will taste like," Simmons said, smiling in Adair's face, exposing teeth that looked like a row of large cloves.

"Come on, Burleigh. Let's git," Slim said. "The damned Army's out and around. And there must be a dozen lawmen looking for us, not takin' account of no Apaches set on killin' every white man in the territory."

31

"Let's kill 'em and git," T.J. chimed in as he pushed back his bowler and scratched his infested black hair.

"Get his britches off, T.J.!," Simmons demanded, pointing the bloody knife at MacLaren's belt buckle.

"Damn, Burleigh," T.J. whined. "You oughten be doin' that, Burleigh. Bible says a man goes to hell fer it."

"You damn fool, T.J.," Simmons laughed, as he fingered the buttons on the fly of his pants.

"But it ain't clean," T.J. insisted.

"It ain't right," Bailey added, always sickened when Burleigh did such a thing to a man.

When MacLaren got the drift of their argument, he'd decided that he'd die and take one or two with him before he let Burleigh Simmons use him that way. While T.J., Bailey, and Simmons argued, Slim kept the Winchester tight to his back.

"Now do like I tell you! Drop his pants!" Simmons shouted, spittle shooting from the corners of his mouth.

The argument was over.

MacLaren felt the muzzle of the Winchester press harder on his back as T.J. reached for his belt buckle. MacLaren was about to spin away from the Winchester when he went wide-eyed with disbelief. The top of T.J.'s head disappeared in a mist of blood, bone splinters, and hair, leaving the black bowler suspended in thin air. The outlaw lurched back, danced a few steps like a horse had stepped on his foot and then suddenly fell into the grass as lifeless as a hundred pound sack of rolled oats. Then, more gunfire from nowhere. MacLaren spun away in time to see the wide-eyed fat man drop the Winchester and stumble forward revealing two, growing red splotches on the back of his shirt. "What?" he said without emotion. "I'm hit."

The one called Bailey went for his gun, but before he cleared leather, two more shots rang out and he backed up several steps and sat down hard, holding his stomach, looking down as blood began to seep through his fingers.

As Bailey was going down, MacLaren dove for Simmons like a man possessed. He drove his shoulders into Simmons' shins. Simmons jackknifed forward and then snapped back, his own momentum sending him flat on his back with his arms outstretched as if awaiting crucifixion.

Though winded by the fall, Simmons still held the knife. Dazed, but still full of fight, he rolled away from MacLaren, and, ended up at Adair's feet. The deputy's feet were chained to the wheel, but he had enough slack to throw several short kicks at Simmons' head. Simmons slashed furiously at Adair's leg, drawing blood. But Adair didn't feel the wounds or stop his frantic kicking. MacLaren got to one knee, and threw himself at Simmons, latching on to his wrist, twisting it with his superhuman strength built on rage and pure animal survival instinct. Simmons let loose an animal sound from deep in his gut as his arm broke with a thump and the knife fell from his hand. In one deliberate, fluid motion, MacLaren snatched the knife from the grass, bolted to his feet, and then fell on Simmons with all of his two hundred pounds, thrusting the big knife into Simmons just below his breastbone.

Simmons grunted and squirmed under MacLaren's weight as MacLaren deliberately worked the knife around in Simmons' chest.

"Kill the sonofabitch! Kill the son..of..a..bitch!" Adair screamed as he strained against his chains, bloody spittle exploding from his mouth. "Gut the bastard!" he yelled, out of his head with anger, drooling streams of bloody mucus.

Simmons wouldn't die. He kept bucking and kicking and nearly dislodged MacLaren several times. Then blood began to gush from the outlaw's mouth. Burleigh Simmons arched his back with a final spasm. The outlaw's eyes focused on infinity, he went limp, and then he loudly soiled himself in death.

MacLaren, still fully charged, jumped up and away from the dead man, taking his dripping knife with him.

"Stay put mister," the kid said, sitting up under the canvas lean-to, his .450 Boxer Colt trained on MacLaren's gut.

Suddenly MacLaren became aware of what had happened. The damn kid had come to and shot Simmons' men. "Listen boy. I'm a U. S. Marshal," MacLaren said, pulling his vest aside to let the kid see the badge.

"I'm shot," Bailey said again.

MacLaren looked toward the outlaw holding his gut and then back toward the kid. "Now lower that Colt, boy."

"Where's my folks and sisters?"

"I'll tell you straight boy. They're gone. Over yonder," MacLaren said pointing to the graves. "To tell you the truth, I'm not sure how you made it, shot up like you were."

The kid sighed, lowered the Colt to his lap, and slowly laid back on the pillow.

"Jesus. God, I'm shot," the outlaw moaned again.

"Get these damn chains off me, Jack," Adair screamed, out of his mind with humiliation and a pain in the side of his head that hurt like someone had stuck a hot poker in his ear.

MacLaren ignored Adair and scanned the ground. He saw what he wanted and fetched his sawed off shotgun from the grass. He walked toward Bailey, thumbing the hammers back as he went, focusing on the sharp pain in his left hand.

"I'm shot," the bewildered outlaw said again, looking up at MacLaren like a puppy dog that had just been run over by a freight wagon.

MacLaren brought the shotgun up and triggered both barrels into Bailey's face, blowing the murderer's head out from under his hat, which hung momentarily in space before taking flight.

"Now you're shot," MacLaren said as he thumbed the breechlock and snapped the twelve gauge open, ejecting the two spent shells in a puff of blue-grey smoke. "Now you're goddamn well shot."

8

Throughout the months of May and June, Victorio and his growing band of Apaches eluded the Army and ravaged the countryside.

After the breakout in which six buffalo soldiers were killed, the
original band had headed northwest, surprising the authorities and
the Army.

After striking small farms and settlements around Santa Fe, they
crossed the Rio Grande and headed south, all the while picking up
warriors from the Mescalero, Sierra del Carmen, and Chiricahua
bands. When they had heard that the Chief had taken to war, others
jumped the murderous San Carlos reservation in search of Victorio's
band, raiding on the way.

They continued to kill and butcher isolated settlers, miners, and
sheepherders as they traversed the Mesa del Oro and headed for the
San Mateo Mountains.

Victorio knew that he and Nana, were flailing at the wind, but it
no longer mattered. Both were out to avenge all the transgressions of
the white man with one final, bloody war. And though, they were
laying waste to only a small fraction of the population in the New
Mexico Territory, people across the territory were jumping at shadows and doubling up on their prayers. A raid killing three miners
would hit the rumor mill and soon turn into the slaughter of a whole
mining camp. The killing of a single shepherd would grow into a
story claiming the lives of everyone in a half a dozen families. Women
talked to each other in hushed tones about the horror of being captured and used by a band Apache bucks.

Units of the 9th Cavalry under Colonel Nehemiah Harper scoured
the countryside for Victorio and his men, but they were no match for
the determined Apaches. Victorio's warriors struck quickly at small

targets and then moved on, easily outdistancing Harper's horse soldiers. The Apaches, on good days, could make seventy miles. They, knew the land and traveled light with fresh horses. The heavily ladened soldiers could never manage that pace.

Victorio intended to strike terror into the hearts of all the white men who were killing off the game, and overrunning his ancient tribal lands with towns, railroads, cattle ranches, mines, and farms. But the blood he was letting was pure retribution. Victorio had set out to avenge the killing of his beloved Chief and mentor, Mangas Coloradas, and to exact payback for the brutal relocation of many of his Mimbres Apaches to hell holes and swamps in Florida.

At the end of June, Victorio struck three families of miners who'd taken up claims on the Blue Creek, just east of Steeple Rock. Without losing a single warrior, the raiding party had descended on the three flimsy cabins in the early morning, killed seven men and boys and, for the first time, taken six women captive.

After three days of riding, they crossed into Chiricahua, Mexico and headed for the Sierra el Tigre, an Apache stronghold for hundreds of years. Victorio's appetite for war and not been satisfied but he wanted to rest, fatten the horses, and give the warriors time to celebrate their success and use their captives. And he longed for one last visit to the place where Mangas Coloradas had confided in him that he would succeed the great Apache Chief.

He knew he would not be pursued into Mexico by Harper's horse soldiers. Until the previous year, the Mexican authorities had looked the other way when U.S. Cavalry crossed the border, but a recent drunken clash between U.S. troops and Mexican troops in a Janos saloon had left two Mexicans and one American dead. The Mexicans had held two U.S. troopers for trial and then hung them. The Army wanted an invasion of Mexico. But the U.S. State Department convinced the President to take no further action and to order the Secretary of War to henceforth honor international boundaries.

Victorio had nothing to fear from the Mexican authorities. No one wanted anything in the Sierra el Tigre and Mexican troops naturally gave the Apaches wide berth. This was especially true for Victorio's band and Geronimo's Chiricahuas. The Mexicans had a natural fear of the Apache and no desire for conflict.

No Mexican soldier would go into the Sierra el Tigre, and any Mexican officer who ordered such a march would have been shot by his men.

* * * *

It was the last day in June when the Apaches began to set camp in the Sierra el Tigre. That afternoon, Victorio journeyed alone to a spot a mile west of the camp. It was a sacred spot for Victorio. He wanted to renew his pledge to his mentor on this piece of land, hoping that the spirit of Mangas Coloradas might appear once again.

In the fall of 1861, eighteen years earlier, the great chief had taken Victorio to this place to tell him that he had chosen Victorio to stand at his right hand. Mangas Coloradas had always shown an interest in Victorio and expected that the skilled warrior would make a great chief, maybe even greater than Mangas.

While the flat outcropping appeared to be nothing more than a piece of sun-parched ground a hundred paces square, for the Chief of the remaining Apache warriors it was a place to recall the past, to remember the tales his ancestors had passed down through the ages, and to reflect on the greatness of his people. Thus it was a place to rekindle his rage. And on this final day in June of 1879, Victorio worked on his rage more than on his memories. As he sat staring into the distance, he recalled the humiliating fate of the great Mimbres Chief, Mangas Coloradas.

In the winter of 1863, Mangas Coloradas had been lured into peace talks under a white flag. Captain E.D. Shireland immediately seized the Chief. Brigadier General Joseph R. West had let it be known to camp sentries that Mangas should not see another sunrise. The guards, overwhelmed with the opportunity to take revenge for fallen comrades, had tied up the old Chief and tortured him through the night with red hot bayonets. Angered when he died, they fired twenty-one .58 caliber rifle slugs into Mangas' body. Still not content, the troopers shot pistol balls into his skull.

A pair of prospectors encamped with Shireland's men had witnessed the brutality and later filed a complaint with General Carelton's Chief of Staff.

A brief Army investigation had concluded that Mangas Coloradas had tried to escape and was shot. The report made no mention of the fact that General West had invited the Mimbres Chief to peace talks under a white flag. Nor was there any note of the dozens of burns on the Chief's body and the grotesque mutilation caused by rifle and pistol slugs.

The story soon made its way to the East, and the death of Mangas became a big story for the reform newspapers in the eastern cities. But most folks in the territories had never given it another thought. For them, Mangas Coloradas was one less savage they would have to kill.

That last day in June, Victorio sat quietly for hours on the very spot he had occupied sixteen years earlier when Mangas Coloradas had confided in him his decision that Victorio would become a Mimbres chieftain. As the sun descended, his rage slowly melted into sorrow and a touch of shame. In earlier days the Apaches were still a great people who could cross their lands without clashing with the white man except on rare occasions. And now it angered Victorio that he was the Chief who had to watch the remnant of his once-great people either die in battle, or worse, become drunken reservation Indians, slaves to the white man's handouts, converts to the white man's god, or whores for the white soldiers. For several years Victorio had privately cursed the Apache gods as bad spirits who would allow such a thing. As the sun set that evening, he settled on the idea that it made no sense to curse the gods because there were no gods looking out for the Apache. There were no gods and no hereafter. There was only today and what he could feel, see, touch, and hear. And death was the end.

9

Jack MacLaren's ranch was alive with people from all over the northeastern part of the New Mexico Territory. Since 1875, Sable Laire Ranch had been the scene of the biggest Independence Day celebration in the New Mexico Territory, a fact more owing to the absolute size of the rodeo, barbecue, and evening fireworks demonstration than to any observance of the 4th of July. Many folks still considered the 4th a Yankee holiday.

MacLaren leaned on a fence rail watching Kriss Andersen hang on for dear life as the horse he'd drawn lurched from the chute. The bay stallion unloaded the kid in two blinks of an eye. The seventeen-year-old boy did a somersault and landed flat on his back. Two riders chased after the stallion and released the bucking strap as MacLaren vaulted the fence and headed for the kid.

But before he'd made it half way across the ring, the kid jumped up, cursing his luck. MacLaren slowed to a walk, suddenly aware that he was acting like a protective mother.

"Anything busted, boy?" MacLaren chuckled, covering his concern.

"Naw, Jack. Knocked my wind out is all," the kid said, disgusted with his performance.

"Don't be so hard on yourself, boy. It hasn't been three months since you were shot twice, once up the side of the head. And you've only been breaking horses for a month. Give it time."

The kid picked up his Stetson, shrugged, whacked the dusty hat on his knee, and headed toward a group of older ranch hands he'd taken to in recent months.

The look that came over Kriss Andersen's face made MacLaren

wish he hadn't talked about being shot. It reminded the boy of the fate of his family. Although the kid appeared to have accepted the reality of the massacre, MacLaren knew that there was a hot fire burning in Andersen's gut. He only hoped the fire would die down before it burned the kid alive. As the kid walked off, MacLaren shook his head and turned toward the fence.

Ever since the kid had gunned down Simmons' friends and saved MacLaren's hide from a certain death, MacLaren had taken a liking to the kid. It was something more than a response to the fact that the kid had saved his life. His feelings toward Kriss Andersen left him uneasy. There weren't a half a dozen people in the world MacLaren counted as friends. And, before the kid, only one person in the world, Mary Beth Lynch, occupied a special place in his life.

MacLaren waved off a friendly greeting from a fellow rancher on his way to the beer kegs as he climbed back through the rails of the fence and took up his position to watch the next rider.

"Jack," a voice said from behind.

"Harley, glad you could make it," MacLaren said as he turned to greet the recently promoted U. S. Marshal. "Come all the way from Santa Fe?"

"I had business in Las Vegas this weekend, so I took up a room at your hotel. Judge Beck sends his best. And his apologies for missing the shindig this year. Said it'll be the first one he's missed."

As Adair spoke, MacLaren marveled at Adair's looks. His six foot frame was lean and normal. But he had the longest face MacLaren had ever seen on a man. It looked like a marble bust started by an artist who quit after only roughing out the features. It wasn't an ugly face, just very different. Word had it that the ladies found him attractive.

Then MacLaren's grin spread from ear to ear as his eyes settled on the lawman's head band.

"God damnit, Jack!" the young marshal said as soon as he saw the twinkle in MacLaren's eye. He didn't know whether to laugh or get mad.

"That headband ain't makin' it, Harley!" MacLaren said as he pushed his hat back on his head and wiped his leathery forehead.

Adair had tried a dozen things to cover the gaping hole in his head which used to be graced with an ear. The latest was a colorful blue headband which had been carefully embroidered by his girl friend with overlapping red and black diamond-shaped designs. Adair wore the band diagonally across his head, high under his hat on the left side, sweeping down just over his eyebrow and around to the side of his head, covering the hole that used to be his right ear.

Adair went red in the face as MacLaren slapped his knee and let out a deep belly-laugh. "Damn, Harley, I liked that flap better," MacLaren said, referring to the leather semicircle which used to hang from the band inside his hat.

Truth was, every time they'd seen each other since that morning they'd narrowly escaped a brutal and humiliating death, they'd both used laughter to overcome the thought of what might have been had Kriss Andersen not come to at that instant in time and shot the outlaws. Not only did the kid awaken at just the right time, but he was also good with a revolver. And to add another dimension to the miracle he'd never shot anything but jackrabbits and rats with his new Colt until that very moment.

Many men are good with a gun, but only a few have the resolve and split-second timing to use a gun on a man. MacLaren's constant kidding Adair about his ear was nothing more than their way of acknowledging that they used up a big chunk of their allotted luck that day in April.

"Hell, Harley. Why don't you just forget trying to cover that up? Considerin' your profession, it might be an asset. It'd be easier to hear the outlaws sneekin' up from behind."

Adair smiled, shook his head and pulled up to the fence. "One thing for sure! It's a reminder, a reminder to never be that careless again."

"I've said that a few times myself," MacLaren added, holding up his hand to reveal the pink stump of his little finger.

"If I ever haul in another one like Simmons, he'll come home ready for the undertaker, not the courts," Adair added, his voice suddenly measured and resonant. "No trash like Simmons ever again gets any slack from me."

"Keep to that and you might draw retirement pay some day, Harley," MacLaren said, always surprised at the changes which had come over his new friend Harley Adair in the recent months. His level of confidence had risen and he'd become the topic of more than one bar room conversation.

"Kid ride yet?" Adair asked, changing the subject.

"Yeah," MacLaren said. "He got thrown hard on his ass. Thought sure he'd busted something. My bones still hurt just from watching him bounce off the ground."

Although MacLaren had never met Harley Adair until the evening he'd locked Burleigh Simmons in the Las Vegas jail, they'd become fast and hard friends. From where MacLaren stood, most young men were frivolous, loud, soft, and stupid with hollow notions about their own importance. But Adair was becoming quiet, competent, and blessed with an understanding of life that no young man ought to have. MacLaren noticed that Adair watched, listened, and learned while most men were too busy talking to ever hear, pisswillies too busy making noise to chase the silence away.

MacLaren and Adair watched another bronc rider go face down in the red dust. The crowd groaned and then cheered the rider as he popped up and limped toward the fence, hat in hand.

"Judge Beck told me to tell you that Victorio and Nana crossed the border and headed into the Sierra el Tigre."

"I already heard. The paper's full of it. Folks are worked up to a frenzy," MacLaren said. "Two of my best hands, Malachi and Joshua, are half Apache...brothers out of a white woman captured before the war between the states. They said they barely made it out of town with their hides one evening last week. Seems like some of the good town's folks were talking about staking them out for a whippin'."

"Folks got to have their demons," Adair answered as if he was talking to no one special.

"The kid's been talkin' about Apaches ever since he settled in here. He can't get enough of it. He hangs on to every rumor like it was a shiny new double eagle."

"Sounds like you've taken up worrin' about the boy," Adair said.

"I've given him a place to stay and hard work at a fair wage. Least I could do, considering he saved my scalp. And yours too!" MacLaren shot back quickly.

"I didn't mean anything by it, Jack! I'm just statin' a fact."

"Guess I have taken to the kid in the past couple of months. Hell, he just turned seventeen a couple of weeks back and he's got more good sense than most men double his age. He'll try anything, work sun up to sun down without complaint, and he gets on good with the rest of the boys, including Malachi and Joshua. And God knows he's good with a revolver!"

"I got no doubts about the way he handles that Colt. Speakin' of that. Did you ever find out where a squarehead kid from New York State learned such a thing?" Adair asked just as a rider finished his ride and received whiskey-soaked shouts and applause from the crowd lining the fence.

"Said his uncle was a gunsmith and crack shot. He taught the boy how to shoot on the sly since the kid's folks were against it," MacLaren answered.

"If we ever get to New York we ought to look that uncle up and buy him a drink," Adair added.

"I guess. Of course his uncle didn't teach him how to shoot men. That can't be taught," MacLaren said. "I don't know where that came from. It bears down on my mind from time to time. I sense the boy's got the will to spill blood without much provocation."

"What makes you think that? The last time I was here you told me that Kriss just woke up that morning and thought he was still in the fight that killed his people. You figured it was a natural reaction. That it wasn't no calculated killin'."

"That's a fact," MacLaren said. "It's things since then. He's always asking around about Victorio and the renegades. I was in the gun shop a week back and Hack Lewis said the boy's already burned out a barrel on that Colt practicing his shooting. Hack also told me the boy buys more ammunition than any twenty men. And aside from a new barrel on the Colt, the boy just spent two months wages on a fancy double from England and then had Lewis cut the barrels and stock down."

"Just takin' after his new pappy," Adair kidded.

MacLaren grunted and offered up a squinty-eyed frown.

"Don't ponder on it too hard, Jack," Adair said directly. "Unless a man's going to be a storekeep or preacher who don't ever set foot outside of town, he's got to be handy with firearms."

"He's been in a couple of scraps in Las Vegas with some of the boys his age," MacLaren went on. "One of them, the Wills kid, called Kriss stupid since he wasn't going to school."

"Christ! Ain't nothin' that schoolmarm's gonna teach that boy!" Adair interrupted.

"I know. But Kriss didn't walk away from the words. According to Billy Wilcomb, Kriss near beat the Wills boy to death. Billy said he kept hitting on Wills long after he was beat. Billy said he saw it all since they went at it right in front of the hotel. Said Kriss never got mad. He just took Wills apart like he was building a fence. I asked Kriss about it and he just said he wanted to do it right the first time so he wouldn't have to fight again. Said he wanted Wills to be a lesson to the other boys."

"Sounds like proper thinkin', Jack. Nothin' to fret over. Boy's got good sense."

"Too much sense for a boy, Harley."

"Hell, Jack! Kriss is seventeen. He's got a few whiskers. He's been shot twice. And he's probably been to Hester Sue's Las Vegas Social Club for a dip or two in the honey pot. Quit your worrin'!"

"I reckon, Harley," MacLaren concluded quietly, a pensive look in his eyes. "I reckon."

They watched the rest of the bronc riders and then MacLaren tried, unsuccessfully, to get Harley to spend the night at the ranch. But the new U.S. Marshal explained that he had to be in Las Vegas to catch the early train to Denver to fetch Kirk Russell from the Denver jail. Russell, was another unreconstructed rebel who'd ridden with Bloody Bill Anderson during the war. In recent years, he'd been a hired killer for several prominent members of the Santa Fe Ring now under attack by Governor Wallace and his new government. Russell, like the rest of the men who'd ridden with Quantrill and Anderson had never been given amnesty. Aside from that old Federal warrant stemming from the war, Judge Beck had three other warrants out, all for murder. Russell was high on Judge Beck's hanging list.

"Be careful. He'd sooner kill you than spit," was all MacLaren had to say as he directed Harley to the iced beer kegs. "I saw him kill a man in a Santa Fe saloon three or four years back. He worked as smooth as a Swiss watch. Shot the man and went back to his whiskey with no more emotion than if he'd brushed off a fly."

10

Jack MacLaren lay awake, staring aloft, seeing nothing. Mary Beth Lynch lay by his side, curled in a ball with her back toward him. Her breathing was slow and steady, her sleep peaceful.

MacLaren's mind was focused on the woman at his side. The last of the visitors who'd been able to travel had left by two in the morning. Several dozen men remained scattered about the ranch, on the ground, in and under wagons and buckboards. Some in bed rolls, others exposed to the cool night, prostrate under the stars.

MacLaren had known Mary Beth Lynch since the first week he'd moved into the territory in 1865. She and her husband had owned Lynch Feed and Hardware, a farm supply house in Las Vegas. They'd met when he had bought a box of rifle cartridges in the store. When their eyes had locked up as he had handed over the four bits for the shells, something happened. He knew at that moment that she would be an important part of his life and she'd later revealed to him that she'd had the same odd feeling. In Jack MacLaren's mind, the union of women and men remained the supreme mystery.

In 1868 while she had been visiting Georgia to settle her mother's estate, the Apaches raided their farm which was three miles west of Las Vegas. Her husband was killed by the raiding party and her two girls, aged eleven and thirteen years, had been carried off and never heard from again.

She had returned to the territory unaware of the fate of her family. The letter bearing the bad news had passed her in the mail. MacLaren, who by '68 had built a friendship with Mary Beth, was one of the territorial U.S. Marshals. Though he was sure that the slightest suggestion on his part would have easily thrown them into a liaison, he never made the move. Morality wasn't an issue. By '68, he'd had thirty-seven summers under his belt, enough to know that butting in on a woman's husband made life more complex than he'd have it.

It was because of his friendship with Mary Beth that folks had pressed him into the job of meeting the stage in Las Vegas and hitting her with the news.

MacLaren had told her directly, and for two weeks Mary Beth Lynch had fallen into a state of quiet depression. No tears. No words of self-pity. She'd just stayed in the small room above the store, slept and stared out the window.

The Army, several bands of militia made up of friends, MacLaren and other U.S. Marshals, and local lawmen had scoured the country-side looking for the girls.

After fourteen days, Mary Beth dressed and went back to work in the store.

"I lost two brothers and my Papa to the Yankees. Tumors killed my mother last month. And now the Indians have taken my family," she'd told him in a matter-of-fact voice later that night over dinner, her piercing brown eyes alive with determination. "Death stalks us and never misses its prey. I intend to take every pleasure I desire and live every remaining day as if there is no tomorrow."

That night in the small room above the store, she'd made love to Jack MacLaren like no woman had ever done before, demanding all the pleasure Jack MacLaren was able to give. Ever since that day, they had been as close as two people can get. Nonetheless, MacLaren had never proposed marriage and Mary Beth had never even hinted that they call in a holy man to say words over their union. As far as MacLaren could tell, she'd never looked back. It was an unwritten rule that the past wasn't a matter for discussion.

The girls were never found. MacLaren had suspected all along that the Apaches had likely kept the girls for several weeks until they'd been so badly used up that they'd killed them and left them for the buzzards and coyotes.

Mary Beth sold the farm and had never laid eyes on it since. She'd built three rooms off the back of the store, decorated them with the best of everything, and had lived there ever since.

As he lay awake, MacLaren's mind continued to race from thought to thought as gray light began to appear in the bedroom window. Mary Beth hadn't moved a muscle. He thought about the kid, about Mary Beth, then on to the fences he was planning on the northeast sector of his range. MacLaren loved fences, long straight fences. He loved planning them, building them, leaning on them with a cool bottle of beer, mending them and painting them. There was something about a long, straight, neat fence that struck his fancy. Whenever sleep was slow in coming, he would focus his mind on fences and that would usually do the trick.

But this night he couldn't concentrate. The kid kept coming back. The kid had struck his fancy too. MacLaren had thought hard on the issue in the previous three months. Though he'd arrived at few conclusions, he had decided that his affection for the kid from Elmira, New York hadn't just come from the fact that the Kriss had pulled his bacon out of the fire. He owed his life several times over to other men and a fine woman, Mary Louise Booker, from Lacy Springs Virginia. And he doubted he felt sorry for the boy because his family had been slaughtered. He'd lost his kin, Mary Beth had lost her whole family between Lincoln's War and the Apaches. Hell, most of the people he'd ever known were dead. He could muster no sympathy for the survivors. He had simply figured that he liked the kid because he saw something special in Kriss Andersen. He saw the raw material from which a man might be molded, a special man, the kind of man who might one day take over his business interests and his land the day he went toes up.

He knew it was the kid that had been making him uneasy in recent months. During the instant when it looked like Burleigh Simmons was about to snatch his life away, he'd felt a certain sense of hopelessness for the first time in his neat and orderly life. All the work he'd done, the hundreds of risks he taken, his very journey back from death during the war, all of it lost to God knows what! He'd never even bothered to make a will, much to the the distress of his lawyer and friend, Judge Harald Beck.

It wasn't some damn fool selfish notion, or some maudlin desire for immortality, it was the conflict it set up in his heart. He'd lived every day since that Yankee pistol ball had knocked him on the head, just for that day. He'd known only that day, that morning, the hour and the minute. The hour that had passed had ceased to exist for Jack MacLaren. And the hour to come was only partly under his control. Any tears shed over the hour past or dreaming about the hour to come were a total waste of time. That wasn't an abstract philosophy for MacLaren. That's how he lived his life.

He was suffering the conflict, staring at the ceiling, because he'd become more concerned about the future that he figured he ought to be.

Mary Beth, still sound asleep, groaned, stretched, rolled to her back, and pushed the sheets down. MacLaren turned and marveled over her thick brown hair and her weathered but elegant features.

47

She never fussed with her hair or wore face paint like most women. She wore her hair down and tied in the back with a leather thong, or in a single braid hanging down, or sometimes coiled and pinned on the back of her head. She rarely wore dresses and never adorned herself with baubles. And she could wrestle boxes and farm implements around her store as well as any store clerk of the opposite sex. Whenever he saw her asleep like this, her hair flowing over the pillow, her body exposed, he knew there was only one woman on earth for him, and he marveled that she was right there before his eyes.

MacLaren turned his pillow over and rolled to his back with a smile from ear to ear. She could do that to him. Most of the men he knew had little use for their wives and were always sniffing after saloon whores, and anything else with a skirt and a painted face. Since his first night with Mary Beth, no other woman had ever turned his head. That was saying something since many had tried, the preacher's wife, the undertakers daughter, and a dozen others. When the ladies of Las Vegas got together to discuss such things, they usually concluded that Jack MacLaren was one of the best catches in the territory. He chuckled over his good fortune and went to sleep as the sun was coming up.

11

MacLaren suddenly bolted upright in bed, for an instant unaware of where he was. The room was warm and the sun high. He looked at the floor clock in the corner and groaned when he noticed it was just past noon.

Jack MacLaren hadn't slept past sunrise a dozen times since the war, no matter how whipped he'd been. He hated to see daylight hours wasted.

After a bath and a shave, MacLaren brushed his wet, sandy-colored hair straight back and turned sideways to the mirror to see if the gray streaks had gotten any bigger. Chuckling to himself over the gray hair, he went to the row of pegs sunk in the log wall, grabbed fresh, black denim pants, and pulled them on. He threaded a wide, supple brown leather belt through the heavy loops on the pants, and hooked the belt with a plain silver buckle inlaid in jade with his brand, SL. He flopped on the bed and pulled on his well-oiled, custom cowhide boots and headed for the kitchen to fill the hole in his gut.

As he walked through the door of the wide open kitchen-dining area, Elaina set a plate of hot biscuits, rare tenderloin chunks, and three eggs over easy at his place on the table.

"Your breakfast Señor Jack. Huevos, carne, y las galletas," she said with a devilish look in her eyes as she poured fresh coffee into his large earthen mug. "Or should I say dinner Señor Jack?"

MacLaren grunted and dropped himself into the leather seat of the big oak chair at the head of the large, simple oak trestle table.

"Where's Beth, Elaina?" MacLaren asked his cook, housekeeper, and part-time mother.

"She and Señor Kriss went for a ride. Dos horas pasado."

MacLaren sliced off a piece of meat, broke the yolks of the eggs,

49

and began devouring the meal as Elaina banged dishes around in the cast iron sink MacLaren had installed a year earlier. He'd built a thousand gallon, forty foot high, red cedar water tower, and installed a windmill-driven pump, he'd ordered from St. Louis. MacLaren reckoned that Elaina fancied that sink with hot and cold water as much as life itself. He'd simply split the incoming water line, plumbing one side of the Y into the hot water tank on the wood-fired cook stove and then from the outlet side of the hot water tank to the tap on the sink while the other side of the Y went to the cold water tap. He'd also plumbed the bath tub off his bedroom the same way with hot and cold water. But to Elaina it was magic. And she understood that he'd spent the large sum on the system mostly to make her life easier.

"Did they say where they were going?" MacLaren asked Elaina.

"No Señor Jack. Just to ride."

MacLaren finished the breakfast and drained his mug. He shoved himself away from the table and popped up feeling energized by the heavy breakfast. He grabbed his dishes and set them on the sideboard next to the sink, put his arm around Elaina and kissed the fifty-year-old woman on the cheek.

"Por Dios Señor Jack!" Elaina said. And then out of nowhere a familiar tune, "When you going to marry Señora Beth and make you both right with God."

"Elaina, I'm sure Mary Beth is already right with God. She is one of His finest creations," MacLaren came back, not the least bit disturbed with Elaina. She was one of those rare people who could say almost anything without giving offense. One could always tell that her opinions were never judgmental.

"You two. You love each other. And the days pass."

"That's true Elaina," MacLaren said as he turned and headed for the door. "Some preacher saying words over us won't change that. Besides, I've seen more love busted up over marriage than for any other cause," he added as he snatched his hat off a peg and disappeared through the doorway.

MacLaren saw his foreman, Joe Harper helping tear down the temporary tables they'd built from barn boards and saw horses.

"Joe," MacLaren said as he approached. "How bad is it?"

"Hey, Jack. Glad to see you up and around so early!" Harper kidded.

MacLaren and Harper had been close friends since his earliest days in the territory. Harper appeared small next to MacLaren, but the little man was tougher than whang leather. Even though he looked older than he was, he was strong and quick and had a reputation that would last him a lifetime.

"Not that much damage this year, Jack!" Harper added. "Things got pretty rowdy too. Must have been more civilized rowdies this year?"

"I guess folks had a good time, Joe," MacLaren said, squinting into the noonday sun. "Looks like you boys will have it put back in shape by sundown."

"I figure," Harper said. "I want to ride out tomorrow for a couple of days and check the water holes. We've been shy of rain so far this season. We might have to start thinkin' on what we might do if it is a dry season."

Joe Harper, like the rest of the people who worked for MacLaren at the Sable Laire, got paid a wage and a share of the profit from the operation. MacLaren took a ribbing from business types in Santa Fe and Las Vegas, but he didn't care. He wasn't about to treat men like business property, like a wagon or a barn.

"Joe, unless you've got a real hankerin' to get off for a few days, I'd like to ride the water holes with Kriss. I've got a few things I'd like to talk over with the boy." MacLaren said.

Until that moment, MacLaren had had plans to spend a couple of days in Las Vegas with Billy Wilcomb. Wilcomb had been after him for weeks to discuss a further expansion of the hotel and saloon. But the chance to spend a couple of days on the range was perfect.

"Hell no, Jack! I'd sooner get at a bunch of chores I've got around here. Be glad to have you do that."

Just as MacLaren was about to ask Harper where Beth and Kriss were, he saw them coming over a rise East of the ranch. By the time he'd finished his talk with Harper, the two riders were dismounting at the horse barn.

As MacLaren approached, one of the hands, the half-breed, Malachi, took Mary Beth's pinto mare off to sponge her down and scrape her dry. Kriss followed Malachi. Both horses needed a washdown and a fifteen minute walk to follow since they'd been pushed into a good sweat under the New Mexico sun.

"Beth, how about a walk to the stream?" MacLaren said as he met her.

"Jack, I'm beat....and hot. Kriss nearly rode me into the ground."

"I saw the horses," MacLaren said.

"Well, I couldn't let the kid get one up on me," she came back.

For a woman of forty-five years, Mary Beth was a horse woman of the first order and, as with everything else she'd done since the death of her husband and the disappearance of her daughters, she'd taken to riding with reckless abandon. At the rodeo the day before, she'd won the barrel racing, outclassing women twenty years her junior.

"Kriss does seem to have a hankering to stay on top," MacLaren said as he gathered Mary Beth's arm and pointed her toward the one mile path that ended up at a clear pool fed by a small stream.

"Jack, I want to cool down and get some water," she protested.

"Clearest water in the territory in that pool," MacLaren answered.

Sensing that MacLaren had something on his mind, she went without further protest. They walked slowly, chatting about the celebration of the day before, taking particular pleasure in some of the antics of their neighbors who'd had too much beer and whiskey under the hot sun.

When they got to the pool, Mary Beth got to her knees and scooped up several handfuls of the cool water and washed her face.

MacLaren chuckled to himself as she wiped her face dry with the sleeve of her faded, red cotton blouse. Somehow Mary Beth Lynch was all woman without ever being dainty, coy, or delicate.

"So, what's on your mind, Jack?" she said as she sat and began pulling her boots off.

"Elaina says we ought to get married and get right with God."

"She says that every time I stay out here," Mary Beth answered as she stripped her cotton socks. "Told me the same this morning. I told her I had no notion of ruining our friendship by standing up in front of some horse's ass in a shiny black suit. The dear woman crossed herself and started banging pots and dishes around in that big iron sink you got her."

"She's a caution," MacLaren laughed.

"Worships the ground you walk on, Jack," she said as she swung her bare feet into the small pool.

"You wouldn't marry me if I asked?"

"Jack, you're not going to ask, so this is foolish talk!" And truth was, Mary Beth Lynch wasn't ever going to marry anyone. Since the day she'd snapped out of her grief, it had struck her that folks are born alone, they live alone, and they die alone and nothing on earth could change that. She'd decided that being alone was the proper order of things and that any interference in that order resulted in trouble. And she'd had her fill of trouble.

That aside, she knew Jack MacLaren was no more interested in a marriage ceremony than she was. They'd had the conversation dozens of times and both always agreed that there was something about marriage that seemed downright silly. Both free thinkers, both beyond the age of dreams, both of independent means, they saw no reason to have the local holy man say words over their relationship. And certainly not the Las Vegas Reverend who was poking one of the girls at Hester Sue's Las Vegas Social Club while his wife was about town offering her favors to more than one man, Jack MacLaren included.

Mary Beth and MacLaren knew that they were joined in a way that no words or ceremony could describe or improve upon.

"How was Kriss feeling today?" MacLaren asked. "Last night he was full of beer."

"I figured you dragged me here to talk about that boy," she said as she undid her blue calico neckerchief and dipped it in the water. "What is it about Kriss that has you so worked up? You haven't been the same since the day you found that boy on the trail."

"Hardly surprising. It's not often a man has a day like that, even in the Territory. Dead people everywhere. Harley's ear chopped off. My finger thrown in the fire. And me near buzzard food," MacLaren said, an odd smile punctuating his words as he thought of Harley's new headband.

"Jack, don't try to put one over on me. I know Jack MacLaren. You're just all worked up because you've gone and gotten yourself attached to Kriss! Hell, you've taken in every stray in the territory, me included."

"I'm not denying I'm concerned," MacLaren said, smiling at her reference to herself as a stray. "I'm concerned about the boy. I'm worried about what he's got up his sleeve. All the shooting he does. That scrap in Las Vegas with the Wills boy. Damn near killed the kid with his bare hands according to Billy Wilcomb. And he's always sniffin' around for the latest dope on Victorio and his renegades."

"What do you expect! Those savages murdered his folks and left him for dead," she answered, her eyes instantly lighted up with the intense hatred she could muster only when talking about Apaches. "Hell, Jack! The boy's just like you. If some murderin' savages had killed your family, you'd have a blood lust that'd scare the Devil himself."

MacLaren didn't answer. He figured Mary Beth was entitled to her hatred for the Apaches. He was amazed at the way she kept it under control and often wondered how she'd fought off the self-pity and depression that would have consumed most women and turned them into nasty old hags over night. And she appeared to have dealt with the missing daughters. Although he knew it was irrational, he'd always imagined that a person had to have a body to put in the ground before they could put a death behind them. Without a body you could never really be sure.

"Jack," she added, her composure regained. "Don't worry on Kriss. The boy's got good sense and some kind of raw understanding about what makes the world work. More than I've seen in some grown men. And he thinks the world of you."

MacLaren looked up at Mary Beth. He was taken aback.

"Of course he's not going to gush all over you, Jack," she added, seeing that she'd suggested something that had truly not entered his mind. "He's been hurt badly and left alone. Funny, here you are dragging me off to talk about Kriss and he's just finished trying to pry information about you out of me during our ride this morning," she said, punctuating her words with her devilish little chuckle.

MacLaren knew that little laugh. When she did that she was having fun at the expense of the ways of men.

"Why don't you just loosen up with the boy," she added. "Pay him some mind."

"Planning to do just that, Beth. It's been too dry so far this season, so I'm taking the boy with me tomorrow to ride the range and check the water."

"He didn't mention that to me."

"I haven't told him," MacLaren said as he got up and moved next to his woman. "Just decided this morning."

"Well for God's sake, don't preach to the boy. Give him his head," Mary Beth said, playfully scolding MacLaren.

"I've been thinking that I'd offer him a piece of the ranch."

"Don't push too hard, Jack. The boy may have other things in mind," she said as she swung her feet out of the water and settled her head in MacLaren's lap.

They were quiet for several minutes and then her presence began to shift his focus. And he saw the look in her eyes. The hot sun burning through the clear sky. The little smile. And the eyes. She could say things with her eyes. Over the years, the sun had taken the youth from her skin. Gravity had altered her shape, and the recent change of life had deepened her voice. But her eyes got more powerful with the passing of time. And right then her eyes were telling him that they were not going back to the ranch just yet.

12

Joe Harper approached Kriss as he was cleaning his tack. "Did you get them horses cooled out and brushed?"

"Yeah, Joe. They're dry and clean. Turned 'em out to graze. Of course they went right down and rolled, undoing all the brushing Malichi and I put in on them," the kid said as he cleaned his bit in a bucket of soapy water.

"Change of plans for tomorrow, Kriss," Harper said. "I'm not goin' out to check the water."

"Damn, Joe. I was looking forward to a few days out under the stars and away from chores."

"You're goin', boy. Just you and the boss."

Kriss Andersen looked up at Harper, somewhat taken aback by the prospect of riding with Jack MacLaren. He had mixed feelings. During recent months, he'd come to respect and admire MacLaren. His reputation was ever present. Everyone Kriss respected spoke highly of him and Kriss had never known a man so generous. Jack MacLaren was a wealthy man but he never held it over anyone. Kriss had never heard of a wealthy man who commanded respect from folks, at least not the kind of respect a man can't buy.

"He told you we're going?" Kriss asked Harper.

"Just before you and Miss Beth rode in," Harper answered. "Hell, boy! Don't look so shocked. It's plain as Harley's missin' ear that the boss has taken a shine to you. And I doubt it's 'cause you shot them trash out on the trail. I reckon he likes you. And that puts you in a special class of folks."

"Well I guess, Joe," the boy answered, his expression revealing a sense of bewilderment. "But what do you figure he wants to take me out for?"

"Probably hoping to have you come to know him better. And that ain't easy for Jack. He holds his feelings close to his vest, boy. Man has to. Nothing worse than a man who don't have enough sense to keep his troubles to himself. I wouldn't give cow shit for a man who wears his misery on his sleeve."

"Some times I don't know how to take the boss," Kriss said. "He seems bigger'n life. Especially to hear the way you and other folks talk. All those stories about when he wore the badge. The men he's killed with that cut-off twelve gauge."

"Most of it is true, boy." Harper added as he pushed his hat back on his head.

"I imagine. I saw him kill that fella Simmons with that big knife and then shoot that gut-shot outlaw so's to take the top of his head clean off."

"You built your own self a reputation that morning. I've heard folks talk harder on that than anything that's happened hereabouts in some time," Harper said.

"I guess. But nobody's said anything to me."

"Probably afraid you're going' to gun them down," Harper laughed as he snatched his hat off and slapped it on his knee.

Kriss looked startled for an instant and then issued a broad smile. "I reckon so," he added, pleased with the reputation he'd never known he'd had until that minute.

"Well, put your things together," Harper said. "Boss likes to ride out before the sun is up. I imagine he'll catch up with you later when he gets back with Mary Beth. I'll see you later, I've got a wagon load of wire and fence posts due in from Las Vegas this afternoon and I've got to make room for it in the equipment barn."

"Where are they off to?" Kriss asked Harper.

"No doubt they're buck naked right now down by the pool and she's ridin' him harder than she rode that mare this morning. Just thinkin' on Miss Beth makes me hard as an ax handle," Harper said shaking his head from side to side.

Much to Harper's pleasure, Kriss blushed bright red and quickly turned away to hang his bridle.

"Women like Miss Beth don't grow on trees," Harper added as he spun on his heel and walked off, still shaking his head.

Although somewhat uneasy, Kriss Andersen headed for the bunkhouse to put his gear in order. Joe Harper had been right when he'd said that most people were not in Jack MacLaren's circle of friends. He'd noticed the signs of MacLaren's concern for his well being, like the way he had vaulted the fence the day before and had run up to him with worry in his eyes.

Within a half hour he had his blanket roll and saddle bags put together. The enthusiasm he put into the task reminded him of the way he and his sisters had concerned themselves with the chore of packing up for their journey West. From the first day their father had announced that he intended to take the family from Elmira, New York to Southern California, Kriss and his sisters had packed and repacked their childish possessions in wooden fruit crates, canvas sacks, leather satchels, and wicker baskets. And each time their father had judged their loads too large for the journey. As he stared at his saddle bags, he felt that those days of childish anticipation had happened in another time.

His mother had dreaded that move while his father had been jubilant over his decision. Kriss recalled his father's excitement because he'd had the same feelings. He often felt poorly that he missed his father more than his mother. She had been a good woman. But her brothers and sisters and her widowed mother were, in his estimation, a bunch of damn loudmouth fools who had devoted most of their waking hours to passing judgment on other people, singling out his father for the lion's share of their abuse. But his father had loved his mother and he had let it pass for years, never countering their carping with any sharp words of his own. "That's the way with folks who live in fear of their own shadows, son," he'd said privately to Kriss after a family dinner at which his grandmother had taken off on his father. "They don't stop talking about others for fear they'll come to know themselves. Just pay that kind of talk no mind, boy. And take it as a lesson. If you ever get to talking others down remember that you'll look as pitiful as your mother's family."

There were still days when he'd look up and expect to see his father standing there ready to explain one of life's complexities or offer up a line of his dry humor. Other times when he was alone he'd say something to his Pa before he'd realize that his father was gone. "Rotten meat in a hole in the ground," he often said under his breath. It had never crossed his mind that his father was in Heaven or floating around in the ether. There had never been a single moment as far back as he could remember when he had believed any of the things he had heard from the lanky, bald Sunday School teacher who used to touch the girls too much and leer too often at their budding womanhood. A man called God? Spirits? A Devil? A hot place called Hell? Walking on water? Parting the seas? "Jonah swallowing the whale," his father used to say. It had all been nonsense to him. But his mother would force them to go, Wednesday nights and all day Sunday. As far as he knew, his father had never seen the inside of a church, a fact that was of particular interest to his grandmother and his aunts and uncles on his mother's side. They'd condemned his father to hell a thousand times. Cursed the ground he stood on. Called him an infidel and worse. And all this time he knew his Pa was more of a man than the whole lot of family detractors. Others in Elmira knew it too. His Uncle Ivan, the gunsmith, and his father's older brother, had told Kriss shortly before they'd left that his father had had enough and that was why they were moving to Southern California.

"Those damn fools got their way," Kriss muttered to himself in the empty bunkhouse. "They drove him off and the Apaches finished the job."

With that he pulled his new Winchester rifle from its saddle scabbard, ejected the 44-70 cartridges and set up his cleaning gear. He was swabbing the clean bore with a swatch of cotton soaked in light oil when he heard the freight wagon coming.

He set down the rifle with the cleaning rod still in the barrel and headed for the door. The load of fencing material had come from Las Vegas and Kriss was hoping for the latest word on Victorio and his renegades. He figured another month's wages and he'd have what he needed to set out to settle accounts with the murdering savage, Victorio.

13

MacLaren was working mink oil into the seat of his saddle when Kriss stumbled into the tack room rubbing sleep from his eyes.

"Looks like another dry day, Kriss," MacLaren said, addressing the boy by his first name.

Hearing "Kriss" rather than "boy" gave him a start, but he worked at not showing it.

"No chance of water from that sky," MacLaren added.

"Hardly tell. The sun ain't up," Kriss answered with a yawn as he turned and snatched a halter and lead rope on the way to fetch his horse from the paddock.

Within the half hour, the ranch was behind them as they rode toward the rising orange semicircle on the Eastern horizon. In minutes the sun began to suck the morning chill from their bones. Deer skittered in and out of the clumps of trees and the birds were making a racket. Lack of rain aside, it was another perfect day.

MacLaren had set a course for several of the small streams, tributaries of the Pecos and the Canadian, which flowed into small pools at depressions in the earth, at sharp bends in the streams, or at natural dams. During a normal year, there was enough melting snow in the Sangre de Christos and enough spring rain to keep the pools full until the summer thunderstorms boiled up and dropped their loads. But it had been a mild winter and a dry spring. Since local thunderstorms were born of the sun and water, there hadn't been a rain cloud in the June sky.

So far there had been no threat to his herds, but without some July rain, there would be serious trouble on the horizon.

"What if it doesn't rain?" Kriss asked MacLaren as they moved on at a fast walk.

"We'll drive 'em to water. Bunch them up on the larger streams," MacLaren answered.

"No doubt every cattleman in East New Mexico will figure likewise," Kriss said. "Be a mess of cows on the rivers."

"There will be a mess a cows going to the yards in Denver, driving prices below cost," MacLaren grunted. "But rain's bound to come. It always does."

"So what are we looking at water holes for?" Kriss asked sincerely, eager to learn what he could.

"I've got to know where I stand long before it's too late to do anything about it," MacLaren said as he dropped his feet from the stirrups and stretched his legs. "If we stay ahead of events, we'll know what we've got to do."

"Sounds like ranchin' puts a heap o' worry on a man," Kriss injected.

"No more than any other way of life. Banker's got worries. Just a different set. Lawman's got worries. Take Harley Adair. Riding to Santa Fe this very minute with that belly-crawling son-of-a-bitch, Kirk Russell. Now there's a worry I'd want no part of. That man's evil in a plain wrapper. Besides, it makes no sense to worry over things you can't control. I'm not worried if it's going to rain. I know it is. I just don't know when. I can't control the rain. But I can control when I move cattle to market or drive them to better water. I can control those things. So you just know everything you can know, turn it over in your skull a few times and make your move. And once you've set your course, you stick with it. A man takes what comes. No tears!"

Kriss nodded, wondering why MacLaren always seemed to make sense. When he spoke, he never wasted words. And most of the time he was quiet. But even when quiet, he seemed to be making a point. One of his looks could say more than most men could get across with an hour of talk. Kriss constantly wondered how it was that their fates had merged that bloody morning several months back. It seemed like years had passed, not months, since he'd shot three men, a fact that had never given him a moment's pause. He'd stepped out of one life when they'd left Elmira. He was just settling into their routine on the road to California, and now he had another life. At times it seemed that he had been living on the Sable Laire all his life.

They walked the horses along the rarely used grassy trail soaking up the morning sun. Both were quiet and neither seemed unnerved by the silence. The scenery made that easy. The rolling hills, the vast expanse of the high plains, and the morning sounds of the wildlife made any talk seem like a crime against Nature.

After three hours in the saddle, they approached a line of cottonwoods. The range was spotted with cattle, their heads down, cropping the browning grass.

"First water is in that stream ahead," MacLaren said, pointing toward the line of trees. "Grass still looks good, though it's going away." With that he nudged Gunn into a strong trot. Kriss followed, his smaller horse breaking into a slow canter in order to keep up.

"We'll have a look around and then move up the creek a bit and put on some coffee," MacLaren said over his shoulder as Kriss pulled along side.

They dismounted at the stream and watered their horses.

"The water is down some, but not a whole lot different from other years," MacLaren said, pleased with the flow of the stream and the level of the natural pool just below. After only minutes, MacLaren mounted up and headed up stream. Kriss followed, becoming mildly annoyed that he was constantly a step behind MacLaren who always seemed to move impulsively.

A half an hour at a walk put them at a grassy area shaded by cottonwoods next to the small stream. Though it was obvious there hadn't been anyone using the site in months, a small circle of blackened stones with grass growing from the center marked the work of earlier travelers. They unsaddled, hobbled the horses, and set them lose to graze.

MacLaren set out gathering fallen twigs and branches and soon had a fire going in the circle of stones and a pot of coffee percolating.

Kriss, content to let MacLaren dash about getting his coffee on, tended his gear, especially his rifle which he'd pulled from its leather scabbard. He wiped the Winchester with a piece of cotton cloth saturated with gun oil and set the new piece against a tree, and then sat down using another tree for a back rest.

MacLaren saw the boy out of the corner of his eye as he fed more dried twigs into the fire. His first thought was that the boy was carrying the gun business too far; then he scolded himself the next instant. Considering what Kriss Andersen had been through and considering the lawless land they were roaming, the boy had the right idea. There was no such thing as being too cautious.

"You must have given a handful of gold for that Winchester, Kriss."

"Thirty-five dollars. It's got the fancy wood in the stock," Kriss answered.

"Does it hold a tight group?"

"Couple inches off the shoulder at a hundred yards," Kriss answered in a matter-of-fact tone, knowing full well only one man in a thousand could shoot that well off the shoulder with iron sights.

"Guess the man holding the rifle has more to do with that than the rifle itself," MacLaren added as he put his hat aside and lay back on the grass, resting his head on his saddle.

"Man who can't shoot, can't shoot with the best rifle ever made. But a wore out rifle of good manufacture ain't much better than the new two-bit, mongrel firearms some stores are selling," the boy answered with an air of certainty attached to his words.

MacLaren was taken with the lad's dissertation and the good sense he once again displayed.

"I've noticed you don't go in for dimestore hardware yourself," Kriss added.

"You'll not get an argument from me," MacLaren responded as he sat up to feed the fire. "There's a lot of junk on the market. I'll not own any of it."

"That's some rig you've got there," Kriss said, pointing to MacLaren's rifle. "Single shot rolling block?"

"Yeah. Remington's Creedmore," MacLaren said. "It'll hold a five inch group at five hundred yards if you can rest it on something. Can't do that off the shoulder. I have hit a deer at four hundred yards off the shoulder, but I always figured it was part luck."

"Damn, that's something! I'd like to try it sometime. I've never shot with a telescope."

"We'll do it in the next few days," MacLaren said.

"You don't carry a side arm." Kriss said.

"I do sometimes when I'm around civilized folk who'd be offended by my stubby twelve," MacLaren said. "Over the years I've come to find out that you're either right up against the enemy or they're way the hell off. That's why I like the Creedmore and the twelve gauge."

Kriss nodded, working the logic of it around in his head.

Both were quiet again. MacLaren wanted to say something to the kid. And Kriss, fully aware that checking water holes was only part of the reason for the trip, waited for something to be said.

When MacLaren did break the brief silence, he simply went on about the flow of the creek, the color of the grass, and the merits of various breeds of cattle.

When the coffee was ready, MacLaren got up, fetched his cup and poured coffee for Kriss and then into his own cup. He leaned up against a cottonwood and took a short sip of the hot liquid. "You know, Kriss," he said, again breaking the silence. "I'm not sure I've ever had the chance to thank you proper for shooting those bastards who were only a lightning flash away from doing Harley and me in. Thanks is about all I know to say. So, thanks."

"Hell, Jack. No need to say anything. What you've done for me is a hundred times better than any words I know," he said, his voice unsteady, his eyes cast downward on his cup. "You didn't have to do all that. Hell, you didn't have to do any of it."

"Understand one thing, Kriss. Nothing I've done is some sort of payoff. More than one man and one fine woman in Lacy Springs, Virginia have kept my soul from the Devil. And I'm thankful for it every day. But I can't say I'd want any of them around on a permanent basis. I'm telling you here and now that you're always welcome at Sable Laire. And it has more to do with the stuff you're made of than it has to do with putting down Simmons' friends. All that, makin' no mention of the fact that you're becoming a top hand who earns his keep and more."

Kriss looked harder at his coffee, fighting back a wave of emotion which was surging through his body. Suddenly, his mind flashed the sight of his father falling to an Apache slug, a scene which had haunted him a hundred times in the recent months. And then Joe Harper's frequent admonition about making a show of one's troubles hit him and brought him back.

"That's about all I've got to say on that," MacLaren said quickly, recognizing that he was choking the boy up. "You're a free man. And if you get a hankering to move on, you do it. Never be afraid to keep your own counsel."

Kriss said nothing. He knew he'd be moving on and he figured that Jack MacLaren knew what he had in mind.

"Like I said before. I thought I was still in the fight with the Apaches when I woke up that morning. I shot on instinct. I don't even know why I shot them and not you and Harley. It wasn't no act of charity," Kriss said, easing his own tension.

His mention of that morning focused the conversation and soon both men broke the serious tone of their short talk with a half hour of graveyard laughs at the expense of the dead Simmons gang, Harley Adair's latest ear patch, and MacLaren's stubby little finger.

But as soon as he'd taken his last swallow of coffee, MacLaren jumped up, poured the dregs of the pot on the small fire, and went to the stream to rinse the pot. He scooped a full pot of water and flooded what was left of the smoldering coals.

They retrieved their horses and were soon on their way. MacLaren said little the rest of the day. Kriss was used to MacLaren's quiet spells so he wasn't unsettled by it. And words of any kind paled in view of the land unfolding in front of them. The deep blue sky met the horizon in a sharp line which magnified the expanse. With a slight breeze at their backs and easy traveling, the ride was pure pleasure. Kriss had come to see that riding alone on the high plains set a man in a state of mind you could get in no other way. The feel of a good horse under you, the knowledge that there was likely not another human being within miles, the absence of man-made noises and the people who make them, and the peace that came from being out of sight of endless chores not done, all set Kriss at peace. Even a short ride on the range usually took his mind off the slaughter of his family and his notions of revenge.

The two riders looked at a half dozen more watering holes, not stopping except for the twenty minutes it took them to eat the fried chicken and fresh brown bread Elaina had fixed the night before.

With four hours of light left, they stopped at a grassy spot within sight of the junction of Mora River and the Canadian. Facing a run-down lean-to there was a large semicircular fireplace built haphazardly of stacked flat stones. As with their earlier camp site, it appeared that man hadn't set foot on the ground for some time.

MacLaren sat in his saddle for a minute and surveyed the situation. "Been two years since I've camped here. Hardly looks like anyone's been here since," he said as he dismounted. "We'll have this place fit to use inside the hour."

Kriss dismounted and went quietly about the business of tending his horse.

It was just shy of an hour when they both stood back and surveyed their work. The beginnings of a fire spat and popped in the refurbished fireplace. MacLaren had fixed the lean-to with several pieces he'd fashioned out of poplar saplings with the small hatchet he always carried in his saddlebags. His oil cloth had been secured over the top of the lean-to and Kriss' cloth was laid out as the floor of the six-by-eight foot space.

"Man could live here forever," MacLaren said as he looked things over. "Kriss, I'm going to fetch a supply of wood. Why don't you take my shotgun and find us a turkey for dinner. You won't have to go far to find one."

"I'll use my rifle," Kriss said.

"Damn, boy, you shoot a turkey with that 44-70 and you'll be coming back with feathers an' asshole and nothing else!"

Kriss smiled at MacLaren, slid his rifle from its sheath, and walked off after his turkey.

MacLaren let loose with a chuckle and then a broad smile. "Boy's got to learn," he grunted to himself as he pulled his knife and set about carving sticks for a tripod and a spit to go over the fire. It wasn't ten minutes before he heard the thunder of Kriss' rifle. He laughed out loud, imagining an explosion of feathers and turkey guts.

MacLaren busied himself stoking the fire, picking up deadwood, and generally cleaning up the campsite. As he was stowing his saddle under the lean-to, Kriss appeared and handed MacLaren a large turkey minus its head.

"I can shoot 'em. But I don't know a damn thing about fixen' one up," he said as MacLaren eyeballed the bloody stump which used to grace a head.

"Lucky shot? Or did you sneak up behind it with your knife?" MacLaren asked.

Kriss gazed confidently into MacLaren's eyes, sheathed his rifle and set the piece under the lean-to across his saddle. Taking a page from MacLaren's book he, thought silence was the right response.

MacLaren added nothing and went about his work, realizing at that moment that he was feeling as close to Kriss Andersen as he had to only a few other people in his whole life.

14

The dawn broke again with not even a wisp of a cloud in the sky. MacLaren awakened from a sound sleep and felt as good as he had in months. As he lay in his bed roll watching the fading outline of the moon he scolded himself for not getting off alone more often.

Kriss lay still breathing steadily and deeply, looking younger and more innocent than he was.

All during the evening before, MacLaren had struggled to find the words and an opening to dissuade Kriss from his obvious damn fool plans to pursue the Apache renegades.

There were times when he thought he had both the words and the cause to launch into a sermon, but something always stopped him and he guessed it was his realization that you can't preach anyone into or out of anything they've set their mind on no matter how foolish, or deadly, or costly it might be.

And he knew damn well that he'd be out for revenge if he was walking in kid's boots. That aside, he was still certain that the kid would end up staked out on an ant hill, or skinned alive, or scalped, or all three if he tried to match wits with Victorio, Nana and their warriors. The thought of it left a black cloud over his spirit.

MacLaren tossed aside his blanket as the first rays of the sun began to warm his face. Stretching his arms over his head, he pondered coffee, bacon, and biscuits cooked over the open fire. The thought got his juices stirring and his stomach rumbling. It wasn't long before MacLaren was up puttering with the fire, the coffee pot, and frying pan.

The commotion awakened Kriss who soon crawled out of his bed roll, stripped off his clothing and headed for the stream with a small block of soap. He spent the best part of a half hour scrubbing himself, cleaning his near-white hair, and just lounging in the shallow, warm water as he scrubbed his undershirt, drawers, and socks.

Later, after they'd finished the bacon and the unleavened biscuits, Kriss surprised MacLaren. "Jack, legend has it you saved the life of Victorio's son. True?"

MacLaren slowly looked up from his coffee. "What makes you ask?"

"Interested is all. Everybody seems to have a Jack MacLaren Apache story," Kriss answered. "I've heard several versions of that one and thought I get it straight from you."

MacLaren was close to letting loose with his sermon but he reined it in. "Don't know as I saved Nana's life. But back in sixty-six, not long after I'd come out here, I was out on the range one day when I came across Nana with a busted leg. I guess he was near dead of thirst. He'd been out hunting and his pony had shied at a sidewinder and gone down hard on his leg. Pony ran off and left the kid stranded. I fed and watered him, and doctored his leg with a splint. Then I rigged a travois and hauled him to the Doc in Las Vegas. Caused a stir I guess. Some folks figured I should have shot Nana like you'd shoot a horse with a bum leg."

"They say Nana walks with a limp?"

"That's a fact," MacLaren answered. "But he still rides like the wind and to hear other Apaches tell it, he's instant death in a fight."

"What happened after you got him to Las Vegas?"

"Oh, his people came several days later and took him off. We were pretty much at peace with the Apaches in those days. There was still room for everyone."

"How did you get friendly with Victorio?" Kriss asked.

"He was beholdin' to me, I guess. After I'd staked out Sable Laire under the homestead law, he came by from time to time. We got to talkin' and tradin' stories. I also came to realize that I'd squatted on land that the Apaches had called their own for hundreds of years. So I told Victorio that his people could always hunt the land and take my beef if they ever came up short of food. I soon found Victorio to be a good and honorable man and called him my friend."

Kriss looked up and met MacLaren's awaiting, penetrating gaze. "Why they're god damned savages!" he growled, his usually smooth face twisted with anguish.

MacLaren had a sudden desire to thrash the boy, but he held himself in check. "They're just folks, boy! Folks at war. It's been going on since Cain and Able. The British and the Yanks. The North and the South. Neighbor against neighbor. And now it's the white man against the red man."

"Jesus Christ a' mighty, Jack! They're just runnin' wild, killin' women and children and babies!"

"Lots of kids and women have been killed in wars, boy," MacLaren added, his voice showing only a hint of distress. "But hell, I'm not going to wear myself down sermonizing. I was twenty years beyond where you are today before it made sense to me. And what finally made sense is that it made no sense and never would. It just is. Like the wind, the sand, and the stars."

Kriss looked up, perplexed at what seemed to him to be pure nonsense.

Seeing the look on his face, MacLaren added, "If that doesn't make sense, get this! If you set out down to Old Mexico looking for Victorio like I know you plan to do, you'll never live long enough to figure anything out. A small band of blooded Apache warriors can go on killing sod busters, tin pans, ranchers, and soldiers for years to come, and you and your Winchester can't do a thing about it. Hell, the U.S. Army can't stop them. They know how to strike and disappear into the Sierra el Tigre where only a madman intent on suicide would follow. The Mexican Army won't even go near there. And Victorio and Nana intend to die fighting. That makes them all the more dangerous. They don't care if they die. Many of those renegades want to die in battle. They fancy it. It beats all hell out of the San Carlos reservation or the Florida swamps. Beside, dying's way down on the list for an Apache. There's a dozen things worse than dying. They don't think like most white men who spend their whole damn lives in quiet desperation, shittin' their pants every day, all because they're scared of dying."

Kriss lowered his eyes to his coffee cup. He knew MacLaren made sense. But he also knew the Apaches were going to pay for his family even if he went down in the effort.

"You corner a grizzly bear, you're going to come up short, boy."

"That's why God made guns, Jack," Kriss said, his eyes still cast downward. It hurt to hear MacLaren call him "boy."

"God gave the Apaches guns too," MacLaren said as he jumped up, tossed the rest of his coffee on the dying fire, and scooped up his blanket all in one sharp stroke.

It was obvious to Kriss that there'd be no more talk about Victorio, or, for that matter, anything else. MacLaren was on the move and it was obvious that the rest of the ride would strain their relationship.

15

Nearly a month had passed without event. MacLaren continued to be amazed at the progress the kid had made. Kriss was hardworking to a fault, smart, and truly becoming one his top hands. Though no one had put a measuring stick on the boy, he'd obviously grown an inch or two since MacLaren and Harley Adair had found him near dead on the trail in the early spring. The hard work around the ranch had muscled Kriss up and the New Mexico sun had turned his hair whiter than ever and bronzed his face. What impressed MacLaren most was the sense of humor the boy had developed and the easy way he got on with the other men, several of whom were three times his age.

Except for the boy's continued practice with his arsenal of firearms, MacLaren had seen no outward signs that he was planning to set out on a suicidal crusade against the Apache renegades. There'd been no talk about Victorio since Kriss had asked him about the chief a month earlier. And Joe Harper, MacLaren's ranch foreman, had relayed the substance of several conversations he'd had with the boy. It seemed that the kid still had a hot fire in his gut, but that his common sense was telling him that he'd be spitting in the wind taking out after the renegades on his own.

All was well. He'd agreed with his partner in the William Bell Hotel to expand the saloon and gambling parlor. His other enterprises were making money faster than he could spend it, so he'd started buying up land on the edges of Las Vegas. He and Mary Beth were spending more time together since she'd found a competent manager for Lynch Feed and Hardware. Even the rain had come, easing MacLaren's mind on that front.

MacLaren had remarked more than once that it was all too good to be true. And it was too good to be true! The serene weeks of July had been the calm before the storm. It was on August 2nd, 1879 that Jason McClintock became the center of a storm that would suck them all into a bloody whirlwind.

On this day, Nana and twelve of his marauders made another of their forays into the Southwestern corner of the New Mexico territory. Although Victorio couldn't forbid the raids, he'd cautioned his son and others more than once about the frequency of their raids.

The renegade band in the Sierra el Tigre had grown to a hundred and fifty men women and children. With the booty from the raids and the plentiful game in the mountains, they were living a tolerable life and one faction within the group was leaning toward settling in to a more peaceful existence before all the men were lost in the fighting. Mellowed by the relative peace of the mountains and the certainty of the ultimate outcome of war with the white man, Victorio was becoming more content to pass the days in the serenity of the Sierra el Tigre. He was concerned for the fate of the women and children, and had suggested that the constant raids could cause the U.S. Army to cross into Old Mexico with a large force of soldiers intent on a slaughter.

But even with the murderous raids executed by Nana, the U. S. Troops had still refused to pursue the raiders into Old Mexico. And Nana, Ciervo Blanco, and others had often brought back gold and silver as well as scalps and white women. Though the Apaches didn't traditionally take scalps, they knew how it terrorized the whites so they'd taken to scalping their victims. The coin and the young captive women allowed them to trade with Mexicans, Comancheros, and white men who all too glad to get whatever the Apaches wanted in exchange for gold and the occasional virgin. The blue-eyed Apache, Cain, had all the contacts and was himself getting rich in the process, a fact that he was not about to reveal to his Apache brothers.

But on August 2nd, Nana raided the wrong ranch. The owners of the spread just east of the Rio Grande and their three daughters and two sons put up a deadly resistance. By the time Nana and his men had overcome the family, he had four of his raiders dead or dying and two more with superficial gunshot wounds which could easily fester into the deadly green death. After five minutes of battle, only the mother, Virginia Burns, was still standing behind a freight wagon, firing with the calmness and precision of a blooded cavalrymen. Then a shot from Ciervo Blanco hit her high on the shoulder and spun her to the ground. Nana rushed the woman, jumped from his horse, and pounced on her with his knife drawn.

70

Virginia Burns recovered her senses in spite of her shattered shoulder and stared into Nana's eyes with a look of hatred and defiance which startled Nana. Ciervo Blanco and several of the others dismounted and surrounded Nana, insisting on their right to violate the woman. Nana agreed and went to pick over the bodies of the dead and get their hair. While she was held down by the others, Ciervo Blanco ripped her clothes off took his pleasure while she strained, spat, and growled defiance as blood pulsed from her shoulder. Ciervo Blanco was evil incarnate. No amount of blood, defiling of women, or destruction of property could satisfy his lust. On more than one occasion, Victorio had thought of executing the deranged Apache, but his fearless approach to battle made him a valuable leader in a fight. While two other Apaches took quick liberties with the woman, Ciervo Blanco held her and carved shallow wounds on her breasts and pulled at her long, fine, auburn hair.

Having ransacked the house and come away with a heavy purse of gold, Nana approached the woman and her tormentors and signaled their departure with a simple sweep of his hand.

In one swift and fluid movement, Ciervo Blanco carved a line on her forehead, jerked her scalp lose from her skull, and then cut the rest of her bloody scalp free from the back of her head. It was so quick that she didn't react until she saw her scalp free from her body. When the pain and horror set in she let lose a primal, scream from deep in her chest, bucking and kicking, dislodging the Apache who was inside her and nearly breaking free from the other who was fumbling for his knife. Ciervo Blanco was about plunge his knife into her chest when Nana stopped him.

"No! Leave her that way," he ordered. "It will give her time to think about death and to know the suffering of the Apache people while she awaits the buzzards."

The Apaches backed away, and the bloody, naked woman got up running on pure anger and lunged at Ciervo Blanco grabbing for her bloody hair. He simply stepped aside, laughing hilariously at the sight of the woman trying to retrieve her scalp. The others joined in as Virginia Burns charged again. But blind fury had carried her as far as it could. She stumbled and went face first in to the red soil, hitting the ground with a thud.

* * * *

The raid had been costly in that Nana had lost four of his best men. More than the whole renegade band had lost since the breakout.

But the final payment was yet to be made. Nana would have done better to kill any other women in the territory save the wife of Governor Lew Wallace. Virginia Burns was the daughter of Jason McClintock.

One of the early settlers in the New Mexico Territory, McClintock was a rancher, and a shrewd, wealthy Albuquerque businessman. Most folks rumored he was the richest man in the southwest. But more important than that, he had the reputation for doing what had to be done, regardless of any formal or informal rules society might put in his way. And whatever needed doing, he did himself. He'd served as a Cavalry officer in the war with Mexico and soon got the well-earned reputation for being a ferocious warrior whether in the saddle with saber drawn or on the ground, hand to hand. In 1859 he'd lost his first wife in an Apache raid on his homestead. That had sent him on a one year rampage to single-handedly wipe the Apache from the face of the earth. Twenty years later, every Apache in the Territory still knew the name Jason McClintock. But time and the demands of business had submerged his blood lust. Nonetheless, most folks figured that he'd still kill an Apache for the sheer pleasure of it if the opportunity presented itself.

To make matters worse for the renegades, they had also killed Jeff Burns Jr., the youngest son of Jefferson Burns, the New York railroad financier.

Early on, the wealthy parents had tried to convince their offspring that they ought not stake out a place of their own in the still-wild Southwest corner of the Territory. Both fathers had offered lucrative spots in their various enterprises and had done everything but shanghai the couple in their effort to keep them close to home. But with the passing of time the parents had come to accept and even respect the independence of their children.

When McClintock got the telegram notifying him only that his daughter had been wounded in an Apache raid, he gathered some of his men and several horses from his remuda and rode the 180 miles to Las Cruces, stopping only briefly to change mounts, water the horses, and gulp hard tack and venison jerky.

He arrived just in time to spend six hours watching his daughter die a horrible death. Tied to the bed, she went in and out of a coma. When active, she strained against the rawhide straps, poured out sweat, and screamed a string of oaths that would have embarrassed Beelzebub himself. At times it seemed her eyes would nearly pop out of her head. It was always obvious that she recognized no one. During her frenzies she would suddenly fall unconscious as fast as she'd jolted awake.

72

Before his daughter died, McClintock had coaxed the details of the raid from Lieutenant Zeke Morrow, the young Army officer in charge of the cavalry patrol that had found the carnage a half an hour after they had heard the first gunshots. By the time he'd heard of the brutal details of the demise of his grandchildren and son-in-law, and witnessed two of his daughter's feverish rages, McClintock had sworn a dozen oaths of revenge.

But when his daughter shook off the head-bandage while thrashing, and he saw the large, putrid oval which revealed the top of her skull, he simply got quiet. His oaths ceased; and all outward signs of anger disappeared. One of the women attempted to rebandage Virgina Burns' skull but found it impossible with her thrashing.

After several more cycles of sleep and feverish rage, McClintock's daughter finally expired in her sleep as he held her hand.

Before the local undertaker had his daughter salted and prepared to travel with the other six corpses, McClintock was burning up the telegraph lines with wires to friends in Albuquerque, Santa Fe, Denver, and Washington, D.C., demanding that the United States send troops into Mexico to track down Victorio and his renegades. This before even notifying Jefferson Burns that his son was dead. But the authorities refused to cross the border, invoking the Janos Accord they'd signed with Mexico, the agreement which had come of the heels of the Janos incident.

The story of the massacre was soon getting headline play in every paper in the Southwest. And the Eastern papers hopped on the story with both feet when they became aware that the dead Jeff Burns was the son of the Jefferson Burns. Any normal family slaughtered by the Apaches couldn't hold a headline but once. But when the rich and the famous were involved, people couldn't get enough of it. Americans took a certain pleasure in the troubles of the nation's natural aristocracy.

Every day new embellishments were added to the story. And with each day, McClintock's rage grew as he and Jefferson Burns tried to persuade Governor Wallace and higher-ups in Washington to run down Victorio. Although the War Department was willing to allocate another company of horse soldiers and ordered stepped up patrols on the U.S. side of the border, it was soon obvious to McClintock that the "God damned chickenshit bastards in Washington and Santa Fe" were not about to break current protocol over a few dead miners and ranchers.

That's when Jason McClintock and Jefferson Burns exchanged a series of telegraph messages in which they decided that they would take care of things the way they would have twenty years earlier, before governments had any say in such matters. And government be damned! Burns was going to catch the first train West and McClintock was to start raising an army right away.

Of course word of their plans got out straight away. McClintock received stern, "official" warnings from Governor Wallace, Judge Beck, and the U.S. Department of State. McClintock paid them no mind. He figured they didn't have the means, the desire, or the guts to stop him, even though his planned foray into Mexico was an obvious violation of federal law. He figured the jawing from public officials was really talk for the Mexican government, that the underhanded politicians would just as soon he put down the renegade Apaches and relieve them of the burden.

McClintock and Burns were out for revenge, pure and simple. They didn't cover that up. By the end of the first week McClintock and Burns had talked to forty men who'd answered their call and picked fifteen of them. They were looking for good men, men they knew, experienced Indian fighters who had more reason than a few double eagles to risk their lives in Old Mexico. They only waived the experience requirement for one man, Kriss Andersen. He'd had to say no more when he announced that he'd quit MacLaren's Sable Laire in order to help hunt down the Apaches who'd slaughtered his family. Most men in the territory had already heard the story of the kid Jack MacLaren had taken in, the kid who'd killed Burleigh Simmons and several of his gang. McClintock was only sorry that MacLaren hadn't appeared to go along with them.

16

A week after the raid which had taken McClintock's family, Jack MacLaren walked into the anteroom of the governor's office with a scowl on his face. Just when things had been looking up, all hell had broken lose. The kid had run off without so much as a "so long." One of his other hands, Kiley Norton, had also drawn his time from Joe Harper and lit out to join McClintock. And now he'd been called to the Governor's office.

He'd contemplated ignoring the governor's invitation, but he understood the workings of politics from his days as a U.S. Marshal. Good politicians never forgot a favor and they never forgot a transgression which bruised their fragile egos. It might take years. But sooner or later they returned favors and always took retribution on transgressors.

He loosened up a bit and a part of his scowl faded when he saw his friends Judge Harald Beck and Harley Adair. Both men were dressed in their Sunday best and therefore looked a little stiff. Adair was sporting a black rig to cover his ear stump. The black cloth ear cover matched his bowler and black broadcloth suit, all of which made his badge stand out like the noonday sun. MacLaren had pondered primping up, but had settled on his tan, flat-brim Stetson, a neatly pressed off-white denim shirt, clean, pressed blue jeans, and a loose-fitting, plain doeskin vest which concealed a Colt Single Action Army revolver secured high on his left side in a shoulder holster. MacLaren rarely went anywhere without his stubby .12 gauge. But when he felt the scattergun would be out of place, he deferred to the Colt which had a three inch barrel and was chambered for .41 Long Colt ammunition. Were the truth to come out, Jack MacLaren had more respect for boomtown whores than he had for politicians. At least the whore was up front in her dealings he'd often reasoned to himself. Politicians practiced the same trade, all the while holding themselves up as a superior class of man. Getting fancied up for the governor was just more than he could take.

"Boys," MacLaren said as he touched the brim of his hat and turned to take a chair next to Adair. "We must be here for the same reason."

"Reckon so, Jack," Adair said, smiling at MacLaren in a way that let MacLaren know that Adair was taking some amusement in MacLaren's displeasure.

"Harald," MacLaren said, nodding to Judge Beck. "What's this all about?" he asked Beck directly.

"Don't rightly know, Jack, but I'd take long odds it's about Victorio and the doin's of McClintock and that New York railroad man who just arrived in Albuquerque. That fellow Burns."

"How do I figure in that," MacLaren asked, his tone of voice revealing some displeasure as being pulled away from the Sable Laire. "Las Cruces is half a world away. I've got no beef with the Apaches!"

"Well let's just hear the Governor Wallace out, Jack," Beck suggested, obviously disturbed by MacLaren's tone of voice.

"The last time you dragged me off the ranch, Harald, I nearly got killed. And because of it, Harley here 'll be wearin' that rag on his head for the rest of his life."

Drawn into the exchange by the comment on his head gear, Adair threw in a couple of barbs of his own.

"Don't you get too frisky, Harley you're still on my list for Kirk Russell," Beck injected, indicating that he was still sore over Adair's conduct in that matter.

While the train had been stopped in Trinidad, Colorado to take on wood and water, one of Kirk Russell's outlaw friends had dressed up as a railroad conductor and tried to free his friend. Adair had come within a whisker of losing Russell and his own hide to boot. But he'd caught on an instant before it was too late and shot the outlaw in the conductor's uniform. Then he'd coldly turned his Colt on Russell, and left the pair to Trinidad's only undertaker with instructions to send the invoice to Judge Beck.

More than once since the Russell affair, Beck had let Adair know that he'd not stand for a U.S. Marshal who executed prisoners.

Adair didn't shrink at the Judge's exhortation. Beck was drawing conclusions. Adair had kept the truth close to his vest.

In the span of six months Adair's confidence had soared and he knew damn well that Beck was unlikely to fire him. He still had two unfilled slots for U.S. Deputy Marshals and no takers on the horizon. As far as Russell was concerned, he'd had fair warning. Adair's encounter with Burleigh Simmons had taught him a lesson or two on dealing with convicted murderers, and caused him to take on a few traits of the timber wolf.

For a half an hour, the three men talked about the McClintock business and speculated on the demands Governor Wallace was about to make of them.

MacLaren was beginning to simmer over the fact that they'd been kept waiting. No one had come out of or gone into the governor's office, not even to beg the Governor's pardon. The business of politics could stir his bile like nothing else.

"Well boys, I guess I'm about to take my leave," MacLaren interrupted the Judge and Adair. "I'll be over at the hotel if Mister Wallace wants to know," he added, getting up.

He hadn't taken a step when the door to the Governor's office opened and a secretary appeared in the doorway and summoned them with his curled index finger and: "The Governor will see you now."

MacLaren focused on the man's finger, wondering how it would look broken off at the knuckle.

Governor Wallace rose to greet them with an extended hand. He was a cut above the average politician and easy to like. A career military man, he'd been decorated in the Mexican War and risen to the rank of Major General in the Union Army during the Civil War. Though his work was for the military and the government, his passion was writing. His first novel, *The Fair God*, had been published in 1873. Though MacLaren hadn't read it, Mary Beth had. She'd advised MacLaren not to waste his time.

"Harald, Harley, Jack," he said as he pumped each of their hands in order.

Each of the three visitors acknowledged the Governor with a cordial greeting.

"Brandy, gentlemen? The day's nearly behind us."

Everyone opted for a drink and they made small talk while the secretary procured the glasses and a crystal decanter. The Governor offered a special thanks to Harley Adair who he was meeting for the first time. Adair took the praise graciously, and much to MacLaren's surprise, Adair seemed perfectly comfortable and dignified in the presence of the Governor. Most people swooned or groveled in the presence of the high and the mighty. To MacLaren's distress, his old friend Harald Beck was doing a bit of swooning. Though their friendship was secure, their relationship had changed since Beck had taken up the bench. MacLaren had often reasoned that the power of the post was wearing away Beck's humanity and sense of humor. He wrote it off to the age old truth that even the best of men couldn't handle unchecked power.

Once the secretary had poured the amber liquid, Wallace waived him out of the room like one might wave off an approaching beggar. Wallace then led them to the corner of the office where an elegantly appointed sitting area had been arranged.

"When's your latest book coming out, Governor?" Beck asked.

MacLaren stirred, knowing Beck hadn't read a book, save parts of law books, since his school days.

"Next year, Harald. Next year."

"You fixed on a title yet?" Beck asked.

"Yes sir. *Ben Hur: A Tale of the Christ*," the Governor answered proudly. "But we're not here to talk about that," he added, suddenly feeling as if he'd been lured beyond the limits of his normally reserved nature. "We're here to talk about this McClintock business. Several days ago I received a long telegram from President Hayes." The Governor cut himself off, rose from the leather chair, went to his cluttered desk, and began rummaging through papers.

"Better yet," he said as he found what he was looking for. "Let me show you."

He walked back over to the trio and slid the telegram across the coffee table to Judge Beck. "Harald read this wire from the President himself. Then pass it on to Jack and Harley."

Beck got the message at once. President Hayes wanted McClintock stopped. He'd insisted that any violation of the agreement with Mexico would have serious consequences. The Apache renegades were Army business. He'd authorized Governor Wallace to take any and all steps necessary to stop McClintock and Burns if they insisted on going forward with their plan to raise a private army to go after Victorio. He warned that McClintock's actions even had the potential for starting a war. He'd closed by stating that he'd had enough of the trouble in the New Mexico Territory, and reminded Wallace that he'd been sent there to fix things, not make them worse.

After each of the men had read the President's telegram, Wallace moved to the edge of his seat. "Gentlemen! I don't know the word failure!" he thundered. "I want McClintock stopped! The man's a throwback. Men like him stand in the way of God's people and their manifest destiny. And God knows, we don't need more Indian trouble. Those cursed eastern papers will build it up and keep people from

78

moving west to the Territory. We need law and order in New Mexico," Wallace concluded, making a sweeping gesture with his arm.

Jack MacLaren suddenly had the feeling that he wanted to be out on his range land planting fence posts in the ground and sleeping under the stars. These sudden mood shifts had frequently overwhelmed him since Kriss had left without a word. Joe Harper had insisted that the kid couldn't face MacLaren because he'd become so close to him and couldn't deal with the fact that MacLaren saw his desire for revenge as a foolish pursuit. Harper had insisted that it wasn't that the kid had been ungrateful.

But hearing Lew Wallace invoking God and Manifest Destiny left MacLaren cold.

"So just tell us what you want," Judge Beck said, breaking a momentary silence. "And we'll oblige."

MacLaren turned his head to catch Beck's eyes. MacLaren's message was clear and conveyed in an instant by his eyes only. Beck didn't speak for him.

"Judge Beck," Wallace said, pointing to MacLaren. "I want you to deputize Mister MacLaren here and send Mister Adair and Mister MacLaren to have a word with McClintock. You tell that heathen that you speak directly for me and that if he persists in this matter, Judge Beck will swear a warrant for his arrest. And Harald, I want you to throw the book at him if he doesn't back down. Put every charge you can think of on that warrant." Then he turned to MacLaren. "Jack, you tell him that if he crosses that border, he'd better stay there, by God!"

MacLaren was about to break in and remove himself from the whole affair, but he quickly realized that there'd be no profit in it.

"Do you understand me, Harald?" Wallace asked the Judge, his voice showing real anger and distress.

"Yes sir, I do," Beck answered sincerely.

"Very well, gentlemen. God be with you!"

17

After an evening of beer, prime tenderloin, and friendly banter at the Los Alamos Hotel in Santa Fe, Judge Harald Beck hadn't convinced Jack MacLaren to put on a badge, but MacLaren had agreed to ride to Albuquerque with Harley Adair to parley with McClintock. After Wallace's "God be with you," MacLaren's tension had quickly disappeared. It was a dead issue. There was no way he was going to pin a badge on, regardless of who asked. But he'd decided there'd be no harm in having a drink with Jason McClintock. Though they were not friends, MacLaren knew the man and had no reason to dislike him.

The following morning they set out for Albuquerque. Though they were traveling light and on good horses, it would be sundown before they'd finish the long ride.

MacLaren had set his mind on simply conveying the Governor's message while offering McClintock none of his own opinion. He understood McClintock and would probably spill some blood himself if he had a daughter done in like Virginia Burns. And though it ripped at his gut, he'd resigned himself to the fact that the kid had a right to his retribution. Though they'd have a number of things going against them, McClintock's little army had a slim chance of putting down Victorio. But he held firm to the idea that the whole damn thing was really none of his business.

MacLaren was quiet as they rode on at a collected trot. Adair knew that any attempt at conversation while MacLaren was in a pensive mood would be wasted wind.

MacLaren was quiet because he was pondering what he might say to the kid. He was also still wondering why he couldn't shake Kriss Andersen like he'd been able to do with most people, including many members of his own family. It wasn't just that he admired the kid's spunk or that they were somehow inextricably linked as a result of the Simmons matter. There was something more. The reason for the bond went deeper. And it eluded him.

After their three days on the range in early July, MacLaren had seen more of Kriss Andersen than in the previous three months. They'd been hunting, out with a crew building fences, and on more than one occasion the kid and Joe Harper had come to Las Vegas with him on hotel business. Mary Beth had taken a shine to the kid and even gone along on one overnight hunting trip. Kriss had also taken up visiting the daughter of the owner of the only store in Watrous, a small pueblo northwest of the Sable Laire. MacLaren had met the girl, and something told him that she was allowing Kriss more than the occasional feel or good night kiss. When Joe Harper offered Kriss unsolicited and explicit instructions on how to tend to the young lady's physical needs he could send the ranch hands into a fit of gut-busting laughter. Kriss took the kidding in stride and often got in a shot or two of his own. It had all been great fun and Kriss was finally laughing, cutting up, and taking an easier approach to life. Nonetheless, he never failed to find time to practice with his weapons. But MacLaren couldn't fault him for that. You could count the serious lawmen in the Territory on both hands. A man had to take responsibility for his own hide if he wanted to hang on to it.

After a pleasant stop at a stage depot for venison stew and biscuits, the afternoon went well as the two men rode the well traveled path under the sunny, clear sky. As was often the case, the pair got talking about everything and anything, including the demise of Kirk Russell. After MacLaren had pumped him for a while, Adair told him what happened.

"I told the son-of-a-bitch when I took him from the Denver jail that I'd kill him if he tried to escape. He did and I held good on my word," Adair said bluntly.

"Lord have mercy, son. Wasn't too many months ago you insisted to reading words from the Bible over the kid's family," MacLaren said. "And now you blow a man's head off without remorse."

"I had remorse," Adair responded in a deadly serious tone. "For about as long as took Russell to shit his pants. I'll tell you, Jack, as long as I have this target on my chest," he added pointing to his badge, "I'll cut no slack for the likes of a Kirk Russell."

MacLaren had observed the changes in Harley Adair with a careful eye and had, reminded him once or twice that there was no shame in turning in his badge if he got tired of the business. He often told

Adair that he had ideas for several business adventures but no good men to see them through. He'd asked Adair to throw in with him a half a dozen times.

MacLaren knew first hand that a man couldn't wear a badge for more than a dozen years at the outside. If some trash didn't backshoot you, sooner or later the nature of the job would twist your mind around so that you'd be looking at life ass backwards.

"Just remember, Harley," MacLaren said as he backed his horse down to a walk. "It's only a job. You aren't God's own personal avenging angel. And no matter how many Kirk Russells or Burleigh Simmons you bring in, there'll be another thousand waiting in line. That's the way it's been since Eve gave Adam a look-see at the old apple."

"I know that," Adair answered.

"Take your Bible and look up those words you read over the graves of the kid's family," MacLaren said as he dropped his feet from his stirrups and flexed his legs several times at the knee. "And this time think on them."

* * * *

The sun was settling on the horizon as MacLaren and Adair stabled their horses in Albuquerque. That tended to, they headed directly for McClintock's White Horse Hotel. It was larger and more finely appointed than MacLaren's William Bell Hotel. Like MacLaren's hotel, the first floor was taken over by card tables, billiards tables, and a large bar. But unlike MacLaren, McClintock kept a string moderately priced whores on the payroll. The night's proceedings were just getting under way as the pair entered the batwing doors and headed for the bar.

MacLaren approached the barkeep and asked for two large draughts. "And then go tell Jason that Jack MacLaren would like to talk to him."

The bartender was about to gruffly deny McClintock's presence when he saw Adair following on, his badge plainly displayed. He didn't know MacLaren from Adam, but he'd heard about the lawman with one ear.

Quickly changing his attitude, the barkeep, drew two beers, thunked them in front of the pair and then scooted under the opening at the end of the bar. The bartender crossed the room at a trot and bounded up the stairs.

The noise in the room faded, and when MacLaren and Adair turned to rest their backs against the bar and gulp the cold ale, it got quieter yet, quiet like when a preacher calls for a silent prayer.

As MacLaren scanned the room his eyes caught sight of Kriss who was backed into a corner on the far side of the room. When their eyes met, the kid touched the brim of his hat.

Though MacLaren's first impulse was to grab the kid, hog tie him and take him back to the ranch over his saddle, he simply nodded and took another long pull on the ale. Before he had done a once-over on the room, he'd taken note of a number of men he'd come to know over the years, former Indian scouts, a couple of retired cavalry troopers, and Ernie Eldridge, a well-known Texas Ranger who'd had his badge pulled after he'd laid the governor of the Lone Star State down with a roundhouse right to the temple. The politician had suggested that Eldridge misplace a murder warrant on one of the governor's crooked supporters. He saw Jeb Hardin, a former Pinkerton man who often free-lanced for the railroads. Then he eyed Frank White, a half-breed Comanche they all called "Chief." Most people agreed that Chief was one of the best scouts in the Territories.

There were others he didn't recognize. But it was obvious that they'd already signed on to McClintock's army. The ones he knew were all good men. If they met the Apaches in neutral territory, there was no doubt in MacLaren's mind that the renegades would quickly go to meet their brothers in the great beyond. But in the Sierra el Tigre, the odds were against them. If they made it back from Mexico, they'd have another battle on their hands. After his meeting with General Lew Wallace, MacLaren was convinced that the Governor would make good on his promise to prosecute the violators. Whether a jury would convict the returning local heroes was another matter.

Only a couple of minutes had passed since the barkeep had hustled up the stairs when McClintock appeared on the landing overlooking the saloon. "Jack MacLaren!" he said loudly. "Get up here, you old rascal!"

The friendly greeting set the room at ease again. Everyone had returned to their games, conversations, whores, and whiskey by the time MacLaren and Adair had mounted the stairs.

"That must be Harley Adair you've got in tow," McClintock said as the pair approached.

"That's right, Jason," MacLaren said extending his hand to McClintock.

McClintock shook MacLaren's hand firmly and then turned to Adair. "Glad to make your acquaintance, son," he said holding out his hand. "Hear you're cleaning up the Territory single handedly?"

"I doubt that, Mister McClintock," Adair said pleasantly as he returned McClintock's firm grip.

After the terse greetings, McClintock turned on his heel and waived Adair and MacLaren toward his personal suite.

Two men were seated in the hallway on either side of the door. It was certain that the duo were not kitchenware drummers.

Once inside, McClintock offered drinks. Still dry from the trail both inquired about another beer. McClintock went right to a fancy oak icebox and got each of the men a pint of MacKensie's Ale. "I have it imported from Scotland," he added as he handed over the bottles.

"Jason," MacLaren broke in as he pushed aside the heavy wire rig which held the cork in place. "Hardly any words that will ease the blow you've taken. I can only say I'm damn sorry to hear about your family. Sorry's not worth much, but it's all I've got."

"Likewise, Mister McClintock," Adair added. "Sometimes it seems like we'll never tame this land."

"Thank you, boys," McClintock said, his back turned as he poured a glass of Scotch whiskey.

"Salud," McClintock said as he turned and held his glass aloft.

MacLaren tilted his beer bottle toward McClintock and nodded before taking a swallow of the cold, dark brew. At that moment MacLaren felt a kinship with McClintock. McClintock was one of the early settlers who'd endured the hardships and did what had to be done to make the Territory habitable. He'd fought Apaches, bandits, and the Mexican Army, chased down cattle rustlers, hung horse thieves, and lost more than one family and dozens of friends in the process. Yet he somehow seemed to have avoided the bitterness that would have crippled most men. For McClintock, retribution didn't translate into bitterness. For him retribution was like accounting, a series of debits and credits that had to balance at the end of the year.

"Damn, Jason. I haven't had a bottle of MacKensie's since Virginia. My father laid up this stuff twenty cases at a time and my brothers and I were breaking into his stock before we were even old enough to chase girls."

"I don't know why you can't get an ale like this here in America," McClintock pitched in. "I've always figured it was because the squareheads run the beer business here. They wouldn't know good ale from horse piss."

Adair chuckled and took another swallow. The dark ale was new and strange to him but not offensive.

"Well, take a load off. Sit down. Tell me what the Governor said. I know you didn't ride all this way to offer condolences and drink my ale."

"That's certain, Jason. Truth be told, General Wallace and Judge Beck sent us to have a talk with you. Or I should say sent Harley to talk with you. I'm not here in an official capacity."

"Ain't no use in tryin' to get me to break my oath to kill the Apache savages that slaughtered my girl and her family. So don't try."

"Well, Jason. We said we'd deliver the message. So why don't you just let us keep our word and listen to Harley here since he's the official visitor."

"You give the badge up?" McClintock asked MacLaren.

"Forever, Jason. I'm set on spending the balance of my years minding my own damn business. Chasing hardcases around the countryside is work for youngsters like Harley here. A man's got to believe it matters to do that work. And chasin' Apaches is work for the Army."

"To hell with the Army!" McClintock blurted out.

"Now, Jason. I know it's asking a lot of you. But why don't you just leave it be. Let the Army tend to Victorio and his warriors. Of course," MacLaren added, "I can't say that I wouldn't be doing the same thing you are right now. But I think I'd also realize that hunting Victorio in the Sierra el Tigre will likely be a suicide mission. And that's a shame. You've still got family depending on you and others counting on you. And I saw a lot of men downstairs I could say the same for. They're good men and they'll follow you because you asked them. That's a heap of weight on your shoulders."

McClintock didn't answer. But his eyes told MacLaren and Adair that he knew that to be the truth.

"Mister McClintock," Adair said, breaking the brief silence. "I guess I ought to chime in and add my piece. First let me tell you that this ain't anything personal. You know my folks and they have always spoken highly of you and your family."

"Nothing personal, boy," McClintock said, hoisting his glass to drain it.

"Governor Wallace says he'll swear a warrant if you cross the border. He showed me and Jack a telegram from President Hayes giving him the authority to use the Army against you if need be. It looks like it's mostly all politics. The damn federal government is getting bigger every day and folks are more often callin' on the government to take care of business they ought to be handlin' themselves," Adair said, using words he'd heard his father speak a hundred times.

"The papers make it all bigger than life, and then your average city folks who couldn't find their asses if they weren't attached read the papers and get to talkin' like a bunch of jackasses. So Hayes feels like he's got to do something, to show folks he's doing something."

MacLaren was surprised to hear such talk from Harley and noticed that Adair seemed to be perfectly comfortable talking to one of the best known men in the Territory. He didn't know the young man had it in him.

"Hayes promised to clean up New Mexico during the campaign," Adair continued, looking McClintock right in the eye. "So far he hasn't done much and his enemies, including some in his own party like Mister Burns, are calling for his scalp. I'm just tellin' you this because I think Wallace intends to make good on his threats even though he and the rest of the politicians would take private delight in you cashin' in the chips on the renegade Apaches."

McClintock stared Adair right in the eye and he suddenly looked even older than his years. The image of his daughter thrashing against the rawhide straps passed through his mind, evoking no anger, just emptiness. "I appreciate your candor, Marshal," McClintock said respectfully. "And I can see that your reputation is built on more than talk."

"Nobody ever said politics made sense," Adair added, again quoting his father, a man who had no use for Yankees, politicians, carpetbaggers, or liars.

With that the room got painfully quiet as McClintock turned to the sidetable next to the ice chest and poured a half a glass of scotch whiskey.

MacLaren finished the last of his ale with a long swallow and signaled Adair by pointing his thumb toward the door.

"If you don't mind, Mister McClintock, I've got other business in Albuquerque," Adair said as McClintock turned with his whiskey. "I'll take my leave now."

"I'll take one more ale, Jason," MacLaren said quickly.

"Go on, Marshal," McClintock said to Adair. "I appreciate what you had to say. And please pass on my best to your mother and father the next time you see them. Your old man's always had his head screwed on straight. I can see it rubbed off."

"I sure will, Mister McClintock," Adair said on his way out of the suite.

McClintock got another pint of beer for MacLaren, and quickly recovered from his momentary vision of his daughter. He and

MacLaren had a few laughs over old times and got caught up on mutual friends who'd fallen on bad times, met up with good times, or gone toes up.

It wasn't long though before McClintock asked bluntly, "What is it you want, Jack?"

MacLaren took a swallow of ale. "You got a boy set on riding with you, Jason."

"Kriss Andersen, the only squarehead in my outfit," McClintock said playfully.

"That's him."

"Hardly call him a boy, Jack. In this country a boy turns into a man pretty quick, especially when he don't have a mama to hold him back. Hell, Bill Cody shot his first red when he was just twelve years old. At thirteen he was helpin' Lew Simpson bull trains to Salt Lake."

MacLaren knew McClintock was right. In the month that had elapsed between the Fourth of July celebration and Nana's raid on the Burns ranch, he'd accepted Kriss Andersen's manhood. But that didn't make the prospect of seeing Kriss dead any more palatable.

"I won't argue that Jason. He pulled my arse out of a serious scrape as I'm sure you've heard. It's just that I've taken a liking to Kriss. I've even had the damn fool notion that I'd pass on part of the ranch to him. Hell, no matter what you or I do the Apache is finished. In ten years this Territory will probably be too tame for either of us. It just troubles me that Kriss, you, or any of those other men downstairs should die for a cause already settled. Regardless of what you do, Victorio will be dead within a year and any Indians left will be the wards of the Indian Agents, a punishment likely worse than death," MacLaren went on. "And if you don't mind, what I said about Kriss stays in this room."

"I won't say anything to the young man," McClintock said, massaging his bald head with his left hand. "What you say about the God damned Apaches might be true, Jack. But it don't mean horse apples to me. I've got accounts to settle."

"I realize you've got to settle up, Jason. And I know Kriss Andersen wants an eye for an eye. It just seems like a damn waste," MacLaren sighed. "I've never had kids and I'll be damned if I don't feel sometimes as if the boy could be my very own. And I wouldn't mind him spending his life on a cause he held dear. But, Jason, to my way of thinking anyone who follows Apaches into the Sierra el Tigre is a dead man, save you going two hundred strong with heavy weapons and such."

MacLaren realized that McClintock's silence meant that McClintock knew he was working on long odds. He also knew Jason McClintock didn't care about odds. He had a score to settle no matter the cost.

"I've already signed Kriss on, given my word," McClintock said. "He seems set on killin' Apaches."

MacLaren understood. A man could fault McClintock on many fronts, but you couldn't question his word.

"Kicking Kriss out of the operation would be akin to a broken promise," McClintock said.

"I understand that, Jason."

"Jack, I'll talk to the boy."

"I couldn't ask more of you, Jason."

18

MacLaren left McClintock's suite, went to the desk and took a room in the White Horse. He'd made the decision not to bother Kriss. He intended to hit the mattress and start out for the Sable Laire several hours before the August sun broke on the Eastern horizon.

He knew that McClintock and his men were going after Victorio and that nothing was going to stop them. It was as certain and final as death itself. The decision to push on had allowed him to quit fretting over the issue. He still had a sore spot in his heart for Kriss Andersen, but he'd truly accepted the kid's fate. Always a loner, Jack MacLaren had told himself more than once in recent days that the kid's departure might be for the best. Personal entanglements had always complicated his life. MacLaren held fast to the notion that when two people hooked up, somebody always ended up on the short end of the stick. He always credited his near-perfect relationship with Mary Beth Lynch to the fact that they each guarded their independence.

MacLaren was beginning to organize the gear he had neatly arranged on his bed when he heard a hesitant knock on the door. He dropped the supple, calfskin saddle bags on the bed, snatched his Colt from the night table, and cautiously answered the door.

Kriss Andersen stood there with a sheepish look on his young face, his bright yellow hair billowing from under his Montana Peak Stetson.

"Howdy, Jack," the kid said, his demeanor revealing that he expected an outburst from MacLaren.

"Kriss," MacLaren said, truly surprised and pleased with the kid's visit. "Come on in, Kriss."

Kriss entered, doffed his hat, and extended his hand toward MacLaren.

MacLaren took his hand and returned the firm grasp. "I'm glad you came by. Have a seat, Kriss," MacLaren added as he waived the kid to the only chair in the room."

"I figured I owed you an apology for runnin' off last week," Kriss said, not moving toward the seat, his words quick and practiced. "Inconsiderate thing to do. And I feel like a damn fool havin' done it."

"Hell, Kriss, you don't owe me any explanation. I figure I understand it."

"I tried to say 'so long' a couple of times and even made it to the ranch house door once," Kriss continued, his voice cracking ever so slightly, his eyes focused downward.

"Put all that away, Kriss. No need for it. I understood. Hell, remember that woman I told you about who nursed my sorry ass back to health during the war. Fact is, I guess you could say I loved that woman. Well....I did her the same way. I couldn't work up the partin' words, so I just rode off into the sunset. I deserted Jeff Davis' army, and I deserted Mary Louise Booker. I always hoped she understood. And fact is, I think she did. It's true enough that there aren't good partin' words for some situations."

Kriss made eye contact with MacLaren and nodded. The tension in the room melted and a knowing smile stretched across the kid's face.

"Now come on," MacLaren said, pointing to the chair. "Sit a spell while I finish fooling with my gear. You know how I like to beat the sun to the trail."

"Yeah I know. It ain't natural. Makes a person feel like he ain't been to bed....getting up before the sun."

MacLaren laughed and returned to reorganizing his bags with the precision of a fine cabinet maker fitting dovetail joints.

"I guess you've heard all the latest," MacLaren said, his demeanor and voice revealing no attempt to talk Kriss out of his plans. "The politicians want McClintock stopped and it appears they're going to try to have their way. Looks like you and your raiders might have to go against the Army, the Governor and his territorial lawmen, and the Apaches."

"McClintock figures the politics is horse shit," Kriss responded, his sheepishness suddenly replaced with his old self-confidence. "He says it's all talk for Mexico's benefit."

"I don't know, Kriss. I was with Harley and Judge Beck when Governor Wallace spoke his mind. And I saw the telegraph from

President Hayes. New Mexico has become a problem for Hayes back East. The papers won't let up on it. Now when you've got a politician cornered and he's only got two ways out and one of them is quittin'....politicians don't quit. The bastards are insecure and vain to a fault. They crave power like a Chinaman craves his opium. So they use that power to fight dirty," MacLaren rambled on, his words coming quickly, spiced with disgust. "Of course there's not one in a hundred who'd fight one-on-one in the street. But corner one of the sidewinders and they'll strike. And they've got legions to do their fighting and a hundred underhanded ways to break a man."

Kriss Andersen's smile faded to a look of concern. He knew MacLaren to be a thoughtful man who was never accused of overstatement. And though he knew nothing of government, other than hearing his uncle call it "God's eternal curse on mankind" at least once a week, he didn't doubt the power of government. But the concern wouldn't translate into backing down.

"Of course I know none of this is going to cause you to quit this damn foolishness," MacLaren said with no malice in his voice or on his face.

"Reckon not," Kriss said quietly as he ran his long fingers through his blond hair. "Mister McClintock already tried to talk me off the venture. I expect you put him up to that."

"You expect right, Kriss. You know my feelings on it. And I understand that you don't know my reasoning. You can't know it until you've got more winters under your belt. Even with the passing of time you'll likely never see it my way. I talked to McClintock because I hate to see a good man under ground before he's had the time to rip off his piece of life and chaw on it for a while," MacLaren said looking right into the kid's eyes.

"I know you're pushin' on what you think's right, Jack. And I appreciate your concern," Kriss answered.

MacLaren thought he detected a wisp of doubt in the kid's voice. And truth was, he had. In the five months the kid had known Jack MacLaren, he had gained some insight into what made MacLaren tick. He'd seen the unspoken respect paid to MacLaren by the people who knew him. He'd noticed that MacLaren was always quietly taking in his surroundings and truly listening to what people said no matter how contrary or stupid their comments seemed to be. He'd seen that MacLaren's simple and highly organized approach to problems small and large usually got things done with a minimum of pain. In those short months, he'd also noticed that MacLaren's off-the-cuff predictions usually came true, whether on the coming of the rain or on the pending demise of Nebrasky Stallybrass, a Las Vegas idler and troublemaker who'd been shot dead for cheating in a card game a week after MacLaren had mentioned the possibility around a campfire one evening on the range.

MacLaren finished rearranging his gear for a quick morning departure as the pair sat in silence. Then he threw his holster over his shoulder, secured the small brass buckles on the straps, and put his doeskin vest on over the blue calico shirt, concealing the holster.

"Let's go down to the saloon and I'll buy you a beer, Kriss," MacLaren said as he lifted the short-barrel Colt from the bed and slid it into the spring-loaded leather holster under his arm. "Give you a proper send-off as you head out to do battle with the forces of darkness," he added with a touch of sarcasm which passed over the kid's head.

"I'd like that," Kriss said as he popped out of the chair and seated his new, light brown, Montana Peak Stetson on his wavy yellow hair.

Once they were at the long, oak bar, MacLaren listened as the kid willingly explained what had transpired and laid out what he knew of McClintock's plans to penetrate the Sierra el Tigre and send the Apaches to Hell's fires.

MacLaren had to admit to himself that McClintock and the experienced Indian fighters in his group had laid out a good plan of attack, at least as good as it could be, considering the circumstances. But none of that changed MacLaren's mind as to the outcome. He calculated that there was only one chance in a hundred that he'd ever see the kid again.

Once Kriss let out all he knew, MacLaren figured he might as well see if the kid was willing to listen to his advice on the matter.

"Considering what you are up against, Kriss, I couldn't add a whole lot. But you'd better understand that you're drawing against slim odds."

Kriss nodded, his eyes revealing that he knew it wouldn't be a Sunday picnic. But there was no doubt that natural, youthful optimism had a firm grip on the young man. At that moment, MacLaren flashed back to the late 1840s when he'd been seventeen. His idea of danger had been losing an arm in the sawmill and the only thing he'd ever killed was fish and fowl. The comparison was startling and caused MacLaren to wonder at what Kriss Andersen had been through in his short life.

"I know I'm buckin' long odds, Jack," Kriss said after a long swallow of beer.

MacLaren's thoughts passed and he turned and looked at Kriss, noticing that the kid could still go several days without a shave before anyone would notice. The gangly seventeen-year-old leaned confidently on the bar as if he'd been sipping beer in saloons for twenty years. It struck MacLaren funny and a toothy smile appeared on his weathered face.

"What?" Kriss asked, seeing the smile.

"Let's grab an empty table and get off our feet," MacLaren said, not answering.

Just as they settled into their chairs, Harley Adair pushed through the batwing doors and scanned the room. On seeing MacLaren and Kriss, he walked deliberately to their table.

"Grab a chair," Kriss said as the young marshal approached, the kid's words showing the first signs of beer.

MacLaren nodded to Adair. He'd hoped to have the kid alone, but Adair's company was always welcome.

After a round of cold beer and a bit of idle chatter, MacLaren broke in.

"Kriss, you ever think that Harley here might have to look you up when you get back from the crusade?"

Kriss laughed nervously and looked at Harley, who was not smiling.

"You'll be bustin' the law just as sure as if you'd robbed a bank, Kriss," Adair added without any malice.

Kriss looked into his beer mug, unwilling to respond.

"No need to fret over getting locked up, Kriss. There's only a chance in a thousand you'll ever get back. And even if you do get back, some drifter will have shot Harley in the back by then," MacLaren added with a grim chuckle.

"After I finish with the reds," Kriss added boldly, "I might just take up with a senorita and stay down in Old Mexico."

The way the kid said it and the fact that neither Adair nor MacLaren had heard such talk from the kid before, set the pair to laughing. Kriss joined in and they were soon laughing off any troubles the future might bring.

With a fresh round in front of them, Kriss broke the carefree mood of the conversation by asking what MacLaren knew of Victorio's past.

"I saw some of those men Jason McClintock has lined up," MacLaren said, skirting the kid's question. "Some have had experience with the Kiowa and the Comanche, but I didn't see anyone who knows the Apache. It's a big mistake to believe that all Indians are the same. The Apache; they're a special breed of Indian. They live for the fight. That's all the men have ever done. They won't herd sheep or cattle, plant the soil, or work for wages. They don't do a lick of work on or around their lodges. They fight, steal, and take their pleasures on their wives. The only work they do is hunting, keeping a sharp edge on their lance, and cleaning their rifle. That's the extent of it. The women do everything else, including the torture of their prisoners. And no people has mastered the art of deception in war like the Apache. Another thing they've got going for them is their code of warfare. They don't have one."

Adair and Kriss Andersen both listened intently as they rarely heard MacLaren expound on anything.

"They'll never attach your strengths. They'll never go against you unless the odds are heavily in their favor. I've know the Apache to follow their human prey for days, even weeks, just waiting for the moment when they have all the odds with them. The Kiowa or the Comanche are fierce fighters and they will come right at you. The Apache is a fierce warrior, but he'll never meet you on your ground. There's the well-known story of Lt. Adam Weber's patrol out of Fort Stanton several years back in '75. Though Victorio said he wasn't party to it, Victorio told me Chato, leading a small band of Chiricahuas, followed the patrol undetected for eleven days waiting for the right conditions," MacLaren said, pausing for a long pull on his draught.

"They'd studied the patterns of the patrol and by the eleventh day they knew exactly where the patrol would make camp that evening. Chato and his warriors had gone ahead and concealed themselves under rocks and in the ground. When the patrol was sleeping, they rose up and killed three sentries and twelve sleeping cavalrymen without a shot being fired. That's the way the Apache will fight you, Kriss," MacLaren said his blue, penetration eyes reaching out from his weathered features and boring holes in the kid's forehead.

"I remember Weber's patrol bein' slaughtered," Adair added. "Word was, all fifteen men were all carved up."

"Scalped?" Kriss asked.

"The Apaches don't usually take scalps. Though they're doin' it more these days since they know the thought of being without hair scares the white man half to death. But in the old days they'd take only one scalp from every raid. The shaman would use it in a scalp dance to purify their weapons," MacLaren answered.

"I recall some of Weber's men were burned too," Adair injected. "Burned after they were dead."

"The Apache finds humor in the grotesque, Harley." MacLaren

said. "What would make you and I toss our dinners can get them to laughing as hard as a person can laugh. They set fire to bodies because they get a kick out of watching them explode."

While Harley chuckled under his breath, recalling the fact that he saw some humor in Kirk Russell's last fart, he noticed that Kriss was finding no humor in the whole thing. A quick glance toward MacLaren showed him that MacLaren was having a good time with the Kid. But he also saw something else building in MacLaren, something he hadn't seen before.

"And another thing; don't trust an Apache woman. Some of their women ride and fight like men. They can be mad-dog mean. It doesn't happen all the time, but some women will ride with a war party. So if you ever get in a scrap, don't ever give a squaw a break."

"And you'd better not let the squaws get a hold of you when they take you prisoner, Kriss," Adair added. "I hear tell they know how to carve up a naked man and keep him alive for days while they're at it."

Kriss listened, and while he believed they were laying it on for him, he didn't doubt what they were saying. He'd been listening to Apache stories for months.

"All this isn't any joke, Kriss," MacLaren added when he realized that the kid thought they were joshing him. "If you get in a fight and you know you aren't going to win it, and you can't run, save your last cartridge for yourself. There's worse ways to go than taking one in the head, and the Apache knows every one of them. I'm telling you straight when I tell you there's no people on earth who get a kick out of torture like the Apache. When I wore the badge, I helped bring back a woman who'd been captured by the Chiricahuas. She'd watched while the Apaches took their good old time killing her husband and son. After stringing him up by his hands so his feet were just off the ground and tying his legs apart with a spreader, the squaws pealed her son's skin, burned his eyeballs with firebrands, sliced his nuts and sausage off, and cut his toes off one by one, all the while laughing so hard they could hardly stand up. For her husband they used their favorite method. You'll always get this one if they have the time to enjoy it. They tie your hands at your side and hang you upside down from a tripod. Then they build a little fire under your skull. Ever so slowly your head begins to heat up. Then you start jackknifing to keep your head from the fire. I hear tell it's the jackknifing that gets them to laughing. Sooner or later, your hair catches fire and burns off. When you are so worn out you literally can't jackknife any more, the heat very slowly gets to your skull and you begin to go insane with the pain. Just when you figure you're going to die and go to Hell, they put the fire out and bring you back, laughing all the time. Then they start over again and they keep it up for as long as they think it is funny. That's sometimes for days. When they get tired of the whole thing one of the squaws will poke a sharp stick up your ass and cut your nuts off. And then they'll stoke the fire and let it go until you die screaming. I guess the final laugh comes after your dead, when your skull finally explodes like it had a black powder charge in it," MacLaren said, obviously a bit in the jug.

Kriss swallowed the last of his draught as if to punctuate the end of MacLaren's tale. He was about to call for another when a drunken drover stumbled and fell on Jack MacLaren. In a burst of disgust, MacLaren flung the man off. The drover stumbled and fell. MacLaren's face got the color of a beet.

Taken aback by MacLaren's unusual outburst, Kriss and Adair suddenly got quiet and then went wide eyed when the drover got up and slapped MacLaren in the back of the head, sending his neat, clean flat-brimmed Stetson to the dirty floor.

With the sudden fury of an explosion, MacLaren spun out of his chair, grabbed a handful of the drunk's shirt and placed three short, powerful right-handed blows directly on the man's nose. The crunch of cartilage and bone and the splattering blood brought instant silence to the large room.

"Jack!" Harley Adair shouted as he jumped up from the table just as MacLaren was about to rip the drover's nose clean off with a fourth blow.

MacLaren checked his punch, dropped the man to the floor, turned on his heel without even a glance at Adair or Kriss, and stomped off, bending over to retrieve his hat on the way.

"Jesus Christ!" Kriss whistled. "I ain't ever seen that side of Jack. What the Hell's come over him?"

"You, Kriss," Adair said quietly as he sat back down. "He's come to care about you as if you were his own blood kin. And he figures the Apaches are about to send you along to be with your folks and your sisters. He can't make sense of it. Hell, this is 1879. The Territory is just about civilized. We'll be a state before long. The Apache is no longer anything but a nuisance. I guess Jack figures you to be the last man to die in the Apache Wars!"

19

MacLaren stepped into the street, tossed his bags over his shoulder, and headed for the stable. There was no moon and the stars were obscured by a thin overcast. It was four in the morning and blacker than the inside of a whiskey barrel. He detected only the faint outline of the odd mixture of adobe and wooden frame buildings which lined the wide street.

He'd tossed and turned in the strange bed which was too short for his six foot, two inch frame. MacLaren had slept for only minutes at a time as his body burned off beer, and his mind contemplated the worst for Kriss Andersen.

But it wasn't just the kid. MacLaren had climbed that summit in life only a few men climb. And when they finally arrive and get a look at the other side, they don't like what they see. During their ascent, they're always hoping for another mountain to climb, something to believe in, something to hope for. But once they reach the top, there's only the distance beyond. They see only a flat, sun-baked expanse with the Grim Reaper waiting at its far edge.

Suddenly the journey seems meaningless. And worse yet, they realize that the trail ahead will be littered with more of the damn fool antics of man.

MacLaren finally found the stablekeeper's door to the left of the large barn door and hammered out his frustrations on the flimsy door.

After a dozen hard raps on the door, MacLaren heard someone growl, "God damn your noise, mister! Hold your water!"

A moment later, the rickety door squeaked open.

"MacLaren. What do I owe you? Gunn, the sixteen hand bay gelding. I'm headin' out early."

"Six bits," the livery owner grunted. "Good bye. And keep it quiet."

MacLaren dropped silver into the man's outstretched hand, fingered a match from his vest pocket, and went through the stable door in search of the lantern.

Once under way, MacLaren kept up a steady pace all morning, resting his horse for two hours just after noon. By early evening, he had reached a line shack on the western edge of the Glorieta Mesa. The twelve by fourteen log shack was on the western side Will Short's Flying S ranch.

Within the hour, he had his horse put up, a fire in the small tin stove, and bacon and beans simmering in the iron frying pan he'd found hung on a nail.

With a full belly, he took his bed roll outside and found a flat spot under a cottonwood only forty feet from the shack. With the first stars appearing and a faint orange glow still visible on the horizon, he fell into a sound sleep in minutes and didn't flinch for eight hours. But for the noise of his gelding cropping grass near by, he'd probably have slept to sunrise in his paralyzed state.

* * * *

At sundown the following day, MacLaren rode into the Sable Laire determined to sink his teeth into business.

He'd decided during the pleasant ride to go to Las Vegas to talk with Billy Wilcomb, his partner in the hotel. Wilcomb had been pestering him to expand, and MacLaren had decided to add on to the hotel and saloon. After settling on a plan with Wilcomb, he was going to set out to talk to some of his fellow ranchers about starting a cattleman's cooperative bank.

Joe Harper and several of his hands were sitting on the small front porch of the bunk house, passing the jug. Joe got up slowly and walked toward MacLaren. "Jack, you look wore out. Let me take your horse."

"Thanks Joe," MacLaren answered, as he dismounted. "I wouldn't want to bust up your little bull session."

"Hell, I've heard all them lies before," Harper said, taking the reins. "I'll tend to Gunn here. You go on in and tend to Mary Beth. She's been a waitin' on you half the day, frettin' like a mother hen."

MacLaren chuckled and let Harper have Gunn. Though it was an unwritten law that everyone took care of their own horses and tack, MacLaren knew that his foreman was pleased to tend to his horse out of friendship and not because he was the boss.

98

MacLaren thumped into his sprawling log ranch house, dropped his bags on the side table just inside the front door, and doffed his Stetson.

He was tired and itching for a soak in the tub.

Mary Beth was seated in a heavy oak rocker looking like she belonged.

Before Mary Beth could speak, Elaina began immediately fussing in her big kitchen at the far end of the open log house. "You clean up, Señor Jack. I will heat the arroz con pollo Señora Mary Beth and I had this evening. I make plenty."

"How did it go?" Mary Beth asked.

"Like I figured," MacLaren sighed as he arched his back to work out a kink.

"I gather Kriss didn't come back with you?"

"Never expected him to. The kid's got his plans pretty well fixed in his skull. He's not going to rest until he draws blood to avenge his folks," MacLaren grunted, still arching his back. "More 'an likely it will be the kid's blood that gets spilled."

Mary Beth added nothing and a sigh of frustration washed over her as she once again pondered the fate of her two girls. The oldest would have been a young woman of twenty-four and she, more than likely, a grandmother. While she usually thought of them as dead, there was that one in a million chance that they were still alive. That slim chance would always deny her the peace that would come from knowing the fate of her daughters.

MacLaren took advantage of her pensive mood to beg off any further talk and head for the tub.

* * * *

After a good scrubbing and Elaina's baked chicken and rice cooked with diced onion and jalipino peppers, he settled into his overstuffed doeskin-covered chair with a glass of his favorite Kentucky bourbon.

Mary Beth had sipped brandy at the dinner table while MacLaren had eaten the feast Elaina had laid before him. But their conversations had only touched on the general goings-on in Las Vegas and the new gossip she'd picked up at her store.

With a fresh glass of brandy, Mary Beth settled into the rocker she'd come to favor. "So what's the latest on Jason McClintock and Burns, the railroad man?" she asked.

MacLaren explained his meeting with Governor Lew Wallace, and, to her surprise, gave her an elaborate account of his evening with

Kriss and Harley Adair, right down to the pleasure he took in busting a drifter's nose.

"You couldn't talk Kriss out of it," she said, not really asking a question.

"No chance. He's fixed on it."

"Did you think to tie him up and bring him back? He's just a kid. I know you are fond of the boy," she said.

MacLaren looked up at Mary Beth, his eyes revealing his frustration. "I've not learned much in this damn fool crazy life, Mary Beth. But I have observed that people are set in their ways and no amount of push and pull from anyone will move them off the road they've taken. Folks take another road only when they've decided on it."

"I know you're right, Jack," Mary Beth sighed, her tongue loosened by the brandy. "It's just such a damned waste. Kriss is a special kid. You go through a lifetime and you're lucky if you latch on to a dozen people you grow to really like. You like them in spite of their looks, their faults, and their opinions on God and politics. Knowing them changes you for the better. Being around them kind of lifts your spirits. It's odd for a young man of seventeen, but Kriss always had a way of setting people at ease with his antics and dry sense of humor. You know, I always noticed how adults always looked on him as one of their peers. They never looked at him as a kid. Hell, I know people in Las Vegas who are twenty-five and they still act half their age."

MacLaren affirmed her words with a nod, and then he drained his glass.

"I'm going to bed," MacLaren announced. "Tomorrow I'm going to see Billy Wilcomb on hotel business and then ride out to see some of the other ranchers about starting a co-op bank. It's about time someone put Bill Finney's fat arse in the fire. His Las Vegas Safe Deposit & Trust has had a monopoly too long."

"Why, that's a great idea, Jack," she said truly surprised by the announcement. "Lynch Feed and Hardware will be your first customer. I can't stand the way Finney is always leering at me. He's a dirty old man."

"Speaking of dirty old men," MacLaren said as he got up and reached for Mary Beth's hand.

"Good night, Elaina," she said, pulling herself up on his hand.

Elaina rolled her eyes back and crossed herself. "You should be married to do that," she mumbled just loud enough for them to hear.

20

Kriss Andersen left Albuquerque with a party of twenty-four men on a five day ride to Columbus, a small pueblo four thousand feet above the sea. Columbus was the intersection of two natural trails, the east-west trail running parallel to the Mexican border and the north-south trail running from Deming in the north, through Columbus, and into Old Mexico.

It had been a slow but pleasant journey as they'd made their way south, keeping the Rio Grande in sight most of the way. Game had been plentiful and the days had been warm and clear.

The men had been in a calm and playful mood, a fact which Kriss Andersen found unsettling. He thought that an impending battle with notorious Apaches like Victorio, Nana, and Ciervo Blanco ought to give them more pause. But no one had paid much attention to him let alone asked his opinion. Had Kriss spent a few more winters on the earth, he'd realized that the men shared his every concern and had a few he hadn't thought of. However, they concealed them with idle chatter, practical jokes, and a devil-may-care facade. McClintock and all of his men had been whistling past the graveyard.

At noon on Monday of the last week of August, they arrived in Columbus with an elaborate chuck wagon, and a freight wagon filled with basic mining equipment. By day's end, they had erected four, twelve by sixteen foot tents on wooden platforms and thrown up a crude corral for their horses. With an eighteen by sixteen foot canvas tarpaulin, a system of polls, and several hundred feet of hemp rope, they had fixed a roof over the chuck wagon, cook stove, and three crude tables made of planks and saw horses. Their camp was nearly as big as Columbus itself.

From their base in Columbus, they planned to support small scouting parties south of the border until they found the renegades. The mining equipment and a certified geologist had been provided by Jefferson Burns. Burns, after consulting friends in Washington, New York, and Old Mexico, had decided at the last minute that they had better provide at least a superficial cover for their mission. His contacts had informed him that the politicians were serious about prohibiting the intended work of McClintock's militia.

McClintock's official posture was that he and his men were looking for silver in the Tres Hermanas Mountains, a creditable cover since there had been several recent silver strikes in the area. Nonetheless, McClintock was still convinced that President Hayes and General Wallace were simply engaging in the crude art of politics with all their threats.

Regardless of the potential for trouble in the New Mexico and Arizona Territories, there would be no interference in Old Mexico. Jefferson Burns had received assurances from his high level contacts south of the border that President Diáz would lose no sleep over the demise of Victorio, and that his troops had been ordered to stay clear of the Sierra el Tigre. Burns and his New York bunch were making large investments in Mexican railroads and Diáz was doing anything he could, underhanded or otherwise, to keep U.S. dollars in Old Mexico. Diáz was staking his future on his foreign investors. Burns and his friends were skittish when they invested beyond the boundaries of the United States. That left them outside their sphere of their political influence. So Diáz was always ready to make concessions.

The next day, McClintock began sending out five man scouting teams who were charged with finding Victorio's stronghold but not engaging any of the Apaches unless they had the clear advantage.

McClintock had gotten off the first team and was seeing off the second when a lone rider appeared on the horizon headed straight for their camp at a slow trot. McClintock, Kriss Andersen, "Chief" Frank White and several others casually set aside what they were doing and picked up their rifles. It wasn't long before they saw the uniform and hardware of a cavalry officer.

The soldier rode up to McClintock and dismounted, acting like he was the guest of honor. "Mister McClintock," he said offering his hand. "How have you been?"

"I'm gettin' by Lieutenant," McClintock said grabbing the soldier's hand. He'd instantly recognized the man as Lieutenant Zeke Morrow, the man who'd found his daughter and her family just after the

Apaches had butchered the lot. He was a short wiry man with jet black hair, a sharp jaw, and a waxed handlebar mustache.

"Glad to hear it," Morrow said. "Mister McClintock, I've got a patrol working just north of here and I ought not stay away, but would you mind if I had a cup of that hot coffee there?" Morrow asked, pointing to the pot on the cook stove. It was almost a command. Morrow was forceful and direct. "And I'd like a word with you in private if I might."

"It'd be my pleasure, Lieutenant," McClintock answered. "You men get on about your business," McClintock said waiving off the four men he was about to send off. I'll see you back here like we planned."

McClintock poured two cups of coffee, handed one to Morrow, turned without a word, and led the soldier to his tent.

"Some mining operation you have here, Mister McClintock," Morrow said once they were inside.

"Yeah, Well," McClintock grunted, his patience beginning to wane.

"General Wallace sent me down here to shut you down," Morrow said directly, his steel gray eyes boring down on McClintock.

McClintock returned the look but with a smile that let the Lieutenant know that it would take more than a phony, determined look to move him off the mark.

"I've got my orders. Wallace has ordered the Army, the U.S. Marshals, Judge Beck, the Bureau of Indian Affairs, and just about anyone else who wants a piece of your hide, to shut you down."

McClintock's face became a crimson mask that would have shocked Old Scratch Himself. "You figure to do all this yourself, Lieutenant?" McClintock growled, his words coming slowly in a gravely measured monotone.

"Nope," Morrow said, smiling, unfazed by McClintock. "I've got forty men yonder, a couple of light artillery pieces, and a pair of Mr. Gatling's latest rapid-fire guns."

McClintock held Morrow's eyes but he couldn't break the soldier. Zeke Morrow had a reputation as a man who never backed away from a fight. Then McClintock's anger subsided as quickly as it had arisen, his eyes fell to his cup, and he turned and sat on his bunk. A vision of his dead, mutilated daughter danced across his mind. The finality of it all had left him emotionless. He had no beef with Morrow, and he knew anger only got in his way.

"Seems like you've also stirred up a hornets nest at San Carlos," Morrow said calmly. "We've been bivouacked at Fort McRae. We got a heliograph from San Carlos two days back. The Apaches on the reservation are all stirred up over you and your bandidos here. The way I hear it, the Apache who takes your hide will be more famous than Geronimo."

"I've sent a few of those God damned savages to the happy hunting grounds, Lieutenant," McClintock said as if he was making idle talk over an ale. "And I still have my skin. They'll be no reds peeling my skin."

"Let's cut through the horse shit, McClintock. Give up this damn fool mining charade. For Christ's sake, the Apache has been beaten. Sooner or later the U.S. Army or Diáz' troops will take care of old Victorio. Hell, there's only a handful of warriors left who haven't drown in pop-skull whiskey, died of the pox, or been sent to live with the alligators. It's Apache sundown. The Apache wars are over."

"Over!" McClintock growled as he stood up and threw his cup aside. "Why you sorry son-of-a...." McClintock paused and ran his fingers once over his bald head. "You saw my daughter and my grandchildren! The war ain't over until the last one of those Apache animals is dead!"

Morrow didn't flinch at McClintock's outburst. He simply finished the rest of his coffee in one swallow.

"I've got my orders Mister McClintock," Zeke Morrow said quietly. "As it so happens, my commanding officer has ordered me to hunt down a small band of Warm Springs Apaches who have bolted San Carlos before I tend to you. Several days back, a dozen of the sorry bastards headed out on half-starved, worn out ponies. No doubt they're out to join up with Victorio. And you're right, I saw what they did to your family. And best we can count, about two hundred and fifty other Americans and Mexicans," Morrow said his voice suddenly permeated with anger.

McClintock raised an eyebrow when he heard the change in the Lieutenant's tone of voice.

"And that's why I'm going to take my time looking for those San Carlos renegades. I'll stretch it out as long as I can. But I'll have to come back. And if you're still here, you and me are going head to head. Damn shame that it is, that's just the way it is," Zeke Morrow concluded. From the moment he'd ridden in, Morrow had obviously intended to cut McClintock a little slack.

"Fair enough," McClintock said, a note of sadness in his voice. "Hope it don't come to that, Lieutenant. I'd prefer to share a bottle of whiskey with you next time we cross paths."

"It'll be on me," Morrow said, touching the brim of his hat just before he turned and ducked through the canvas flap of McClintock's tent."

McClintock stood quietly, listening to Morrow ride off, his mind a jumble of disconnected thoughts. His daughter thrashing deliriously against her tie-downs. The first family he lost to the Apaches, their images blurred by the passage of time. Pompous, grotesque politicians, all Johnney-come-lately's who'd slithered into the territory now that it was tamed. Bureaucrats in Santa Fe writing rules and regulations that turned a free man into a ward of the state. Pisswillie settlers who looked on a six shooter with the same fear and loathing they reserved for a six foot diamondback. He was becoming an anachronism; and he knew it.

He slumped into a moment of self pity, dwelling on the fact that he and the other men who settled the territory would never get a footnote in the history books, while the political hacks who washed in with the tide would get all the glory.

But digressions into self pity didn't last long for Jason McClintock. A smile spread over his face as he had the thought which often lifted him from a momentary funk. He knew that he was one of the handful of men who ever got the opportunity to live as he had, to be as free as the wind, to survive or perish through the exercise of free will. Freedom wasn't handed down by politicians and their laws, their very existence squashed freedom. Freedom was the freak union of a unique place, a hardy breed of people, and a fleeting moment in time. It was a state of nature that struck only a few times in recorded modern history. He'd been struck by its magic. He'd known a life most men could never even imagine as they made their slow, monotonous march toward their graves.

The thought invigorated Jason McClintock. He bolted from his tent burning with a new desire to accomplish his mission.

"Dorsey, Chief, Eldridge, the rest of you boys!" McClintock shouted like a drill sergeant. "I want you boys saddled up in fifteen minutes!"

21

Kriss Andersen, Frank "Chief" White, Ernie Eldridge, Jeb Hardin, and Dorsey Bowles had been out for two days. They'd crossed the border at Las Palomas, a sleepy little pueblo in Chihuahua. After quizzing several people in town about Victorio and his people, they had nothing more to go on, so they headed southwest toward Janos through Boca Grande and El Espia. After a day in Janos, they'd collected all the rumors in town and headed due west.

The men had come to know one another in the several weeks since they'd first signed on with McClintock's bunch. Four of the five in their group had become close friends, Dorsey Bowles being the outsider.

Frank White was a half-breed Comanche who'd taken to the ways of the white man as the Comanche wars subsided. But the men still called him "Chief." Ernie Eldridge was the former Texas Ranger who'd loosened the teeth of the Texas Governor when the Governor insisted on a political favor which insulted Eldridge's honor. Jeb Hardin was the former Pinkerton man who'd done odd jobs for Jefferson Burns. Dorsey Bowles was a quiet man with fifty winters under his belt. Bowles had a reputation as an Indian hater and a Indian killer who was simply in the fight to draw Apache blood. McClintock and Bowles had known each other for over twenty years. Bowles was in charge of the five man patrol.

They'd had two unproductive days and nights since leaving Columbus.

They set out on the third day with a mind to turn north and scout the Hatchet Valley.

Before taking the lead, Bowles reminded them again that the Apache was the master of the ambush and that they were to be especially watchful in places where an ambush appeared least likely.

Kriss and the Chief spread out to the left, while Hardin and Eldridge scouted the right flank.

They'd only been working the valley for two hours when Bowles came up over a rise riding hard toward them.

"About a mile dead ahead," Bowles said as he met Kriss and the others in his party. "Ten Apaches heading due south, headed straight down Hatchet Valley?"

"War party?" the Chief asked.

"Looks like it. No women or children and they're travelin' light. Though I wouldn't say they look fit for no war," Bowles grunted as his horse nervously spun around.

Kriss felt his heartbeat quicken with anticipation. "What do we do Dorsey?" Kriss asked.

"I know how we can kill 'em. If we ride steady, there's a spot where the valley narrows just west of Hatchet Peak. 'Bout five hours from here. It's real rough either side of the trail and hardly a white man ever lays eyes on the valley. I figger those reds will be unawares goin' through the pass. That's where we'll kill the sorry bastards. Like shootin' frogs in a pond!" Bowles laughed as he reined his horse around and prodded the beast into a lope. The others looked at each other with raised eyebrows and shrugs, and then kicked their horses in behind Bowles. It was the first time they'd seen Dorsey Bowles fired up since they'd met him. He was suddenly acting like a kid on his first deer hunt.

* * * *

When they reached the ambush site, Bowles and the Chief automatically took command and quickly found five positions which would conceal a man and his horse.

Unsure of the progress of the Apaches, Bowles moved quickly from position to position, giving his orders. Kriss, Hardin, and Eldridge didn't question the Chief and Bowles who appeared to have the situation in hand.

"Wait until they are right in front of us. Then open fire from your position. The Chief and I will start from the front of the pack and work back. Kriss," Bowles ordered. "You, Ernie and Jeb shoot from back to front. Shoot them and their ponies. When them's that left start to scatter, mount up and run the devils to ground. Don't give 'em no quarter. Not even the blink of an eye. Don't get all wrought up and waste your shots. Aim and shoot. And be careful! I ain't diggin' no graves."

Kriss was at once excited and concerned about what lay ahead. Shooting a turkey or a deer was one thing. Shooting men and horses was something else. He'd once watched Joe Harper shoot a sick old horse back at the Sable Laire and the sight of it nearly caused him to toss his dinner. Oddly, he caught himself worrying more about shooting an Indian pony than an Indian. "Like shootin frogs in a pond!" Bowles had said. But the image of the four graves in which Harley Adair had planted his family was never far from his mind when he needed it. He was certain he'd take his revenge, and he was bolstered by the fact that all five of them had killed men before, though it didn't seem real that he'd killed three of Burleigh Simmons' gang. That had been quick and unplanned and he'd been shy a portion of his senses.

For over an hour, the five men laid in ambush, becoming more convinced with the passing minutes that they had missed the Apaches. The sun was beginning its rapid journey west, and a gentle breeze had come up to ease the afternoon heat.

Kriss was scanning the distance as Jack MacLaren had taught him during one of their hunting trips. He'd pick a single place in the distance; hold that spot and look it over. Then he'd shift his eyes to another area and hold. And so on. MacLaren had insisted that if you keep your eyes and head moving, you miss most of what's in front of you.

Kriss was staring at a point in the distance when he saw riders on the horizon. They were Apaches. The sight sent a charge through his body which tripped his heart off and caused his face to flush red. He thumbed back the hammer on his Winchester, and looked toward Jeb Hardin the only one he could see. Hardin had also seen the Apaches.

Time seemed to slow as the Apaches walked into the ambush. They were now close enough for Kriss to count ten bucks and fifteen horses. Kriss was becoming unnerved at the lack of caution displayed by the Indians. He wondered who MacLaren was talking about when he gave his lecture on the cunning and stealth of Victorio's men. The sorry Indians were talking loudly, and paying no attention to the trail in front of them. They had no one scouting ahead and their rifles were sheathed.

Kriss felt faint as his juices coursed through his veins. His pounding heart almost hurt. The trailing Apache was only a hundred yards from their ambush. The nickering of one of their horses or the glint of a rifle barrel could set it off. He had his sights on the last Indian in the bunch.

Kriss suddenly remembered his reins and secured them under his belt. The first shot could have sent his horse into battle without him. His horse secure, he sighted on the trailing Indian. As they continued forward at their leisurely pace, Kriss saw that he had his sights on a scrawny kid who looked half starved and grubbier than one of Elaina's hogs back at the Sable Laire.

The lead Apache was now abreast of their trap and Kriss, still sighted on the kid in the rear, was feeling weak in the stomach and beginning to wonder what the hell was going on. Wasn't anyone going to shoot? As suddenly as the question passed through his mind, the Chief and Bowles opened up on the lead Apache. Kriss squeezed the trigger of his Winchester. The rifle cracked and he saw his slug hit the Apache square in the chest just as the Indian's horse bolted, giving the appearance that the Apache had been blown twenty feet backward off the horse by a stick of dynamite.

Suddenly the air was thick with gunsmoke, as the five bushwhackers methodically jacked round after round into their rifles and fired on their prey.

Apaches and horses went down. The sickening sounds of lead hitting flesh and bones, frantic, squealing horses, and dying Indians sounded like a symphony played in Hell.

After Kriss Andersen had killed the kid, he'd paused and stared out over the rocks fixed on his victim. He hadn't fired a second shot. The Indian kid rolled slowly over on to his side, pushed himself up on one elbow, looked around, and slowly settled on to his back, the heel of his right foot rhythmically pushing at the ground.

As Kriss stood, his eyes still fixed on the dying kid, Bowles and the Chief emerged on their horses, their revolvers drawn. Eldridge and Hardin followed. There were still six Apaches on their ponies who had collected themselves and were making a run.

Bowles and the Chief took off after the two who'd raced south beyond the ambush site. Jeb Hardin charged the remaining four, but went down in a heap as he was fired upon by an Apache who was covering for the trio in retreat. It was the first shot they'd gotten off.

Kriss, still at his position and suddenly aware that he had frozen after his first shot, quickly sighted the Apache who'd fired on Jeb and hit him dead center, but high of his mark. The slug caught the Indian in the neck and Kriss saw the Apache's head turn halfway around as his pony spun and danced, finally throwing the buck to the ground. Seeing Ernie Eldridge hot on the trail of the three who escaped to the north, Kriss came to his senses, jammed his Winchester in its saddle scabbard, mounted his dancing horse, and rode out after Eldridge.

Certain they were not going to outrun their pursuers, the Apaches left the trail and headed off into the rough terrain. Eldridge followed the one who'd bolted to the west. Kriss followed the remaining two who'd headed east. While he was still breathing hard and could feel his heart slamming against the wall of his chest, he had started to think more clearly. His senses were heightened in a way he'd never imagined possible. He almost felt like he was floating rather than riding. Caution was the word frozen in his mind as he headed up the rough slope. His view straight ahead was good, but his view to the top of the ridge was obscured by a the old growth spruce trees. But he kept on, sure the Apaches would continue to run.

As he climbed a rocky knoll, he broke out of the trees and saw the two Apaches urging their ponies up a steep, rocky incline.

Without thinking, he jumped from his horse, hauled the Winchester from its sheath, and drew a careful bead on the trailing warrior. He squeezed of the round and the Apache went backward off his horse. The other Indian, stopped and turned. Seeing his friend down, the young buck jumped from his horse and ducked down toward his friend.

Kriss, still running on instinct, took careful aim and fired two more rounds, killing both the Indian ponies.

The other warrior, another skinny Indian, barely on his way to manhood, stood up defiantly and looked down on Kriss Andersen as if to dare him to shoot. Kriss sighted a perfect shot on the Indian's breastbone, but couldn't take it. It was easier than frogs in a pond. Too easy. The Apache didn't even have a weapon.

The young Apache, turned and ran. Kriss Andersen would later regret letting his easy target get away.

Kriss, suddenly drained from the ordeal, tied his horse and walked carefully up through the rocks toward the spot where he'd shot the Apache. He was half way up when a shot rang out that nearly caused him to jump out of his drawers. Then he realized it was probably Ernie Eldridge.

When he reached the narrow ledge, he saw the Apache who was down. He was an older man. He had a big rip in his belly and his entrails were hanging out. He was mumbling and still had life in his eyes.

Kriss looked around frantically as if he might find a doctor or someone to help save the Indian. And then it hit him that the man on the ground might have been the kid's father.

The dying man looked up at Kriss and tried to lift his hand to make a sign.

Kriss drifted into a trance as he stared down upon the mumbling man.

The sound of a horse coming toward him quickly brought him back, and he turned to see Jeb Hardin coming up through the rocks on an Indian pony.

"Jeb!" Kriss said, plaintively. "We got this man shot!"

"I guess he is," Hardin chuckled.

Then Kriss remembered that he'd seen Jeb go down when he'd charged out of his ambush. "Jesus. I thought you were shot!"

"Red devil shot old Junior right out from under me. And we both went down. Best damned horse I've ever owned."

Kriss forgot the wounded Apache for a moment pondering how Jeb must feel about his horse. Jeb Hardin loved that Chestnut gelding. But the gurgling and moaning brought him back to the wounded Apache.

"What do we do?" Kriss asked Jeb.

"Leave him for the buzzards," Hardin growled. "I hope he lives long enough so's he can watch the buzzards eat his guts."

"Christ, Jeb. We can't do that."

"He's gut shot, kid."

"Jeb!"

"Piss on the red devil. Let's get back. The boys might need our help," Hardin growled, as he turned the pony and headed back down the slope.

Kriss looked down at the Apache. The Indian's eyes locked on to his and Kriss saw into the man's heart. He saw no malice, no pain, only a plea for help. He drew his Colt and fired, sending the Apache to Kingdom Come.

It was all he could think to do.

22

The young Apache, Mano Suerte, ran until dark, driven on by the words of his dying father, Lanza Roto. Like all Apache men, he obeyed his father. Certain he would never survive his wound, Lanza Roto had insisted that his youngest son escape the white men and find Victorio's people to tell them of their breakout from San Carlos and to record their fate in the Hatchet Valley. He wanted someone to know that they had rejected life on the reservation and left this world fighting like men. With his final words he commanded his son to find his older brother Ciervo Blanco, and to ride with him to kill the white man.

After two days of walking and running, the young Apache was intercepted by two of Victorio's men riding guard on the perimeter of their stronghold in the Sierra el Tigre. Already weakened by the brutal life at San Carlos reservation, Mano Suerte was exhausted and starving.

Dorsey Bowles and Chief watched from a concealed spot on ridge a thousand yards away as the Apaches retrieved the parched Mano Suerte. They had been trailing the Apache since the ambush in the valley. When they had regrouped after the short slaughter, Kriss had lied to the others about why he had let the Indian go. He had explained that they might be able to trail the kid to the Apache camp. Bowles had complimented the kid for his quick thinking and he and Chief went after the boy, leaving Kriss, Jeb Hardin, and Ernie Eldridge to tend to the mess which resulted from their ambush.

* * * *

Ciervo Blanco was in camp when his younger brother was brought in.

112

On hearing of his fathers's death at the hands of the "White Hair," Ciervo Blanco started a commotion which brought Victorio and others from their odd assortment of crude lodges.

As he had done countless times over the years, Victorio again confronted Ciervo Blanco and insisted that he check his temper. Victorio saw in the warrior's eyes the hatred and the inherent wickedness which was burned into Ciervo Blanco's spirit. But the fearless warrior was insistent. He wanted to assemble a raiding party at once to avenge the death of his father.

While Victorio or any other chief or shaman could not prevent Ciervo Blanco or anyone else from building a war party, as a chief, he was at least entitled to be heard at a council. And Victorio usually got his way, winning over his warriors with his regal stature, his intelligence, and his ability to see the bigger picture. His noble appearance alone made him a natural leader. And they all knew that Mangas Coloradas himself had passed on his authority to Victorio. But most importantly, Victorio had earned their respect by his spectacular feats of cunning and bravery in battle.

Victorio insisted on a meeting, but Ciervo Blanco kept talking. Victorio reasoned with him once more, this time letting Ciervo Blanco have a dose of his penetrating eyes, a sure signal that Victorio had heard enough from the agitator. The Apache Chief had a stare that unsettled most men, red or white.

Without further protest, the bloodthirsty Ciervo Blanco agreed to a council that evening. Victorio said they would hear from Mano Suerte on the fate of Lanza Roto and they would discuss a plan to avenge the death of Lanza Roto. He surprised the warriors who'd gathered by adding that he had new information on the hated McClintock.

* * * *

Chief White and Dorsey Bowles had trailed Mano Suerte and the two careless Apaches who'd rescued him. The Apaches had led McClintock's militiamen right into the Sierra el Tigre. They had ridden into what appeared to be a canyon with no exit. But there had been a way out of the maze. It was hidden by an optical illusion. But, once you'd found it, the trail out was as plain as the nose on your face.

Once through the canyon, Bowles and Chief had decided to stay put, fearing a higher concentration of sentries beyond the exit to the strange canyon. Chief had insisted that they move further only under the cover of darkness. Chief was certain that Victorio's camp was close by.

* * * *

Seated around the fire with the leaders of Victorio's renegade Apaches, Mano Suerte told his story. He recounted every detail from the breakout at San Carlos to the point where he was found by Victorio's men. He explained his father's last words and how he had stared down the muzzle of the "White Hair's" rifle and how the spirits had interfered with White Hair and prevented his death.

The story of the ambush of Lanza Roto and his war party saddened and angered Victorio. He was saddened by the loss of friends. He was angered that the Apaches had become so soft and stupid that they would wander into an ambush like lambs to the slaughter. But the tales of life at San Carlos left the Chief with emotions that went beyond sadness and anger. The tales of San Carlos left him hopeless and drowning in despair. San Carlos had always been hell, but the obvious criminal misappropriation of food, clothing, and money allotted to the Apaches during the winter and summer of 1879 had left the reservation Apaches starved and robbed of the last remnant of their dignity.

Mano Suerte said that he, his father, and the men who'd joined them were the last men with any fight left in them. The others, he said were drowning in whiskey which made them sick as well as drunk. Even the women had taken whiskey. And the youngest maidens were given to whoring for the soldiers at Fort San Carlos, some for whiskey, but most traded their dignity and honor for food and clothing for their families.

Ciervo Blanco was quiet. But as he stared into the dancing flames of the council fire, he was nearly insane with his desire for the blood of the white man.

When the skinny and tired Mano Suerte had finished his story, Victorio asked Cain to tell the council what he had learned.

Cain was the half-breed son of an Apache shaman and a white missionary woman snatched in a raid near Fort Yuma in 1852. But for his blue eyes, Cain looked pure Apache unless he was decked out in his odd assortment of clothing and the mammoth sombrero he wore when he hung around Janos and other towns in the Territories and Old Mexico. In that getup he looked foolish. Cain's specialty was setting up trades with Mexicans, comancheros, and white men who would hand over their sisters for a few pieces of silver. The half-breed traded captured gold, silver, and jewelry, for rifles, ammunition, food, and other necessities.

The blue-eyed Apache got on well with the Mexicans. They were scared to death of him. Cain was always pleasant, courteous, and businesslike unless he was crossed. No one who crossed Cain, lived to brag about it. The Mexicans called him El Machetazo because of the large machete he carried. Rumor had it that Cain could dismember an enemy quicker than most men could clear leather with a six shooter.

Cain explained to the council how he'd been in Janos when five white men came to town asking about Victorio.

"I recognized the killer Bowles and the Comanche, Frank White. I have never seen the others," Cain said. "But I tell you Mano Suerte, there was a tall white hair. Very Young. From hearing you, I say this 'White Hair' is the one who killed your father."

"And the father of my brother, Ciervo Blanco," Mano Suerte added.

Ciervo Blanco looked up and nodded to his frail looking little brother, but added nothing to the conversation.

"No one in town talked," Cain added with a toothy smile.

It was an observation which gave them all great pleasure. They hated the Mexicans as much as they hated the white men, and they respected them less.

"McClintock's men." Victorio said to the others seated around the fire. "That man lives for Apache blood. We know of his plan to see every Apache dead. My son, Nana, and Ciervo Blanco killed his family and his daughter's scalp hangs in Ciervo Blanco's lodge. That is good. But now we will have to kill McClintock. His power is great among the white men. Cain tells us of Dorsey Bowles and the Comanche dog, Frank White. I know these men. Bowles kills because he likes killing. The Comanche kills for gold. But I know nothing of this White Hair."

Ciervo Blanco for the first time during the council, demanding that they make a war party and run McClintock and his men to ground. In minutes he had the council hot for war.

Victorio let Ciervo Blanco go on for several minutes and then heard from several respected warriors who thought it prudent to stop the raids and enjoy the fall and the winter in the Sierra el Tigre. After listening to everyone, he held his hands up requesting that order be restored.

"The great Chief Victorio is not going to ask us to sit here like squaws, is he?" Ciervo Blanco growled.

Victorio shot a cold look at Ciervo Blanco, a look which brought instant silence to the council. Then the Chief looked down at the fire. They all sat for several minutes and heard only the noise of the fire.

"Your blood runs hot Ciervo Blanco," Victorio said calmly, breaking the painful silence. "And I fear it is not just for the loss of your father, Lanza Roto, a man of wisdom, a great Apache warrior. I fear that you have the lust for blood in your spirit, the same power that sickens a white man like Dorsey Bowles. If a man kills to overcome his enemy it is the defeat of the enemy which is the objective. Killing is merely one step along the path to the objective. We kill a deer to eat. The objective is to achieve victory over hunger. We do not kill a deer to watch it bleed. When a man kills only to satisfy the evil spirits within, that man is a danger to all because his vision is obscured by the blood in his eyes."

You could have cut the tension in the air with Cain's machete. Several at the council were sure that Victorio was only moments away from killing Ciervo Blanco. Most in the renegade band admired Ciervo Blanco's spirit and willingness to fight, but no one saw him as a man of wisdom or a natural leader. They knew that Ciervo Blanco's lack of patience had gotten them in trouble on several occasions. Were Ciervo Blanco to defy Victorio, he'd do it alone. That was understood by all.

Nana intervened and broke the tension. "Ciervo Blanco, let us hear from my father."

"We will not sit like squaws," Victorio said after another moment of silence. "Ciervo Blanco is right. McClintock must be killed. But we would be fools to fight McClintock and his men on their terms. And we are not fools," he said, turning again to fix his eyes on Ciervo Blanco. "An Apache who would throw away his life is a fool. Our fathers taught us the ways of war, and their fathers before that. The purpose of war is to kill your enemy. And we will kill our enemy as our fathers would have killed our enemy, with the cunning of the fox, the quiet approach of the eagle, and the ferocity of the brown bear. That is how we will kill McClintock, the killer Bowles, the White Hair, and the others."

23

Harley Adair rode toward the Sable Laire under a cloudless, morning sky. The temperatures had fallen to near freezing the night before, an unusual occurrence for the first week in September. The crisp weather, the endless landscape, his best horse under him, and the morning sun in his face all made for one of those days that can usually lift a man's spirit, no matter the burdens he carries.

But this dazzling first Saturday in September served up by a Mother Nature in good humor didn't put Harley Adair at ease the way it surely would have a month earlier.

The Thursday morning past, Judge Beck had called him to his office in Santa Fe. The Judge had angrily ordered Adair to join up with Lieutenant Zeke Morrow and arrest McClintock and any of his men within reach. "I want that son of a bitch here in my jail," Beck had shouted, thrashing around his office like a caged mountain lion. "I don't care whether they're brought to me in irons or stacked up in a wagon like cordwood," he'd said as he thrust a stack of warrants in Adair's face.

It had been barely a week since the ambush of the ten San Carlos Apaches in the Hatchet Valley. The newspapers in every town were full of it. People across Arizona and New Mexico were talking about nothing else. Jason McClintock and his militiamen were heroes to most folks. All but a few Quakers and Yankee missionaries were pleased to hear that more Apaches had gone belly up. Victorio's renegades, according to the current tally had killed over two hundred and fifty people in Old Mexico and the Territories since their spring breakout.

Though the five men who'd killed the Apaches didn't know it until later, their ambush had occurred just over the border in the Arizona

117

Territory, a fact which added a new dimension to the problem.

To make matters worse yet, McClintock had insisted that his men bring in the nine bodies of the dead Apaches. By the end of the week, every paper had artists' drawings of the nine bloated corpses. And several itinerant photographers had made their way to Columbus. They were selling photographs of the grotesque, disfigured bodies. Folks were giving a day's wages for a photograph.

All this had infuriated General Lew Wallace. Jason McClintock and his men had thumbed their noses at the law; they were making a laughing stock of the territorial government. It was salt in the wound that McClintock had close ties to the still active Santa Fe Ring, all of whom were having a great public belly laugh on Wallace's account, using their paper, the Santa Fe Morning Times, to lionize McClintock and mock Wallace. When Wallace had seen the artists' drawings reproduced in the Morning Times and read how McClintock's men had hauled the Indian carcasses back to their camp in Columbus, he'd been truly offended. Wallace was a Bible-believing man who held stock in an all-powerful, vengeful God. He could deal with the sting of unflattering editorials and cartoon caricatures, but the desecration and display of the Apache bodies was a gross insult to the God he knew.

Adair had been truly taken aback by the ferocity of Judge Beck's ranting and raving. Beck had always been thoughtful, calm, and reasonable in their previous dealings.

But Wallace had unleashed his fury on his military commanders and Judge Beck. And Beck had shoveled the whole load on Adair and the other territorial marshals.

His immediate reaction to Beck's unchecked anger was to tell Beck to put on his own God damned pistol and go and get McClintock if he was so set on having him in jail. But he'd held his tongue, and escaped Beck's office at the first lull in the Judge's protracted sermon.

Adair had made previous plans to escort a prisoner from Santa Fe to the Denver & Rio Grande Station in Las Vegas where the rail line ended. Further rail construction was still held up by political skulduggery. There, the Denver police were to take charge of the killer and bank robber to haul him back to Denver on the evening train for a speedy trial and hanging. He hadn't mentioned that fact to Beck, but he'd had no intentions of heading off to find Zeke Morrow's U.S. Cavalry until he'd delivered his prisoner as promised.

His prisoner safely in the hands of the Denver authorities that next evening, Adair had had a half dozen mugs of ale and a good night's sleep in MacLaren's William Bell Hotel. Awake before sunrise that

Saturday morning, Adair had saddled up and headed away from Jason McClintock, the pueblo of Columbus, and the trouble that went with it.

Unsure of his reasons or purpose, he'd headed east toward the Sable Laire. As he rode toward MacLaren's spread he had time to puzzle it all out. Early in the week, life had made sense. This Saturday morning, his life had suddenly and mysteriously seemed pointless. He'd worn the badge for less than a year. In that time he'd made the transition from blissful innocence to first hand knowledge of the darkest side of man. He'd killed men, one of whom was unarmed and chained to the floor of a railroad baggage car. He'd watched his own certain death occurring right before his eyes, only to have the Grim Reaper run away at the last moment, making off with only an ear. Until he'd pinned the badge on, he'd only taken quick pleasures with a few farm girls. Now he couldn't go two days without being offered the opportunity to lay with voracious women who knew all the ways to turn lose the animal in him.

And now all this. He had no beef with McClintock. Like McClintock, he was of a mind to see the Apaches gone once and for all. As far as he was concerned, McClintock had every right to avenge the death of his family, and he couldn't see that it was any of his business to step in. He certainly had no intention of paying back Kriss Andersen for saving his life by hauling him back to Beck's jail.

When he saw the sprawling, log ranch house and numerous out buildings on the horizon, he finally decided that his detour to the Sable Laire had been a good thing. But he still didn't really know why he was there. He liked Jack MacLaren more than any other man he had known, save his own father. He always felt safe and happy in MacLaren's presence.

When he rode up to the barn, Jack MacLaren, Joe Harper, Malichi, Cass Dixon and several others were shoeing horses.

"Harley," MacLaren shouted over the noises of the forge bellows and the clanking of Cass Dixon as he pounded glowing steel into a horseshoe on a large anvil. "What the devil brings you out here? Locked up all the scofflaws in the Territory and come for honest work?"

"Not likely, Jack," Adair said as he dismounted his sturdy paint. "Never be an end to outlaws. Just when you thing you've got it done, the government makes more laws....makin' more outlaws."

MacLaren laughed. He was always in good humor when working around the ranch. But he sensed that Adair was carrying a load on his shoulders. "What's the matter, Harley? You look like you've been scorned by a woman or lost your dog."

"Shows up that bad, does it?"

"Joe, take Harley's horse here and put him up. I'll drag him over to the house for some of Elaina's lemonade," MacLaren said to his foreman. "Can't think straight with all this commotion."

When they went inside, Harley was surprised to see Mary Beth.

"Why Harley," she said as he came through the door. "What brings you out here?"

"Oh well, Miss Mary Beth, I had a few things on my mind, things I'd hoped to pass by Jack," Adair said as he doffed his Montana Peak Stetson and hung it on a hat peg beside the massive oak front door.

MacLaren went to the kitchen end of the house in search of lemonade. Before MacLaren even got started, Elaina emerged from the pantry and began scurrying around and scolding MacLaren for messing around in her kitchen.

The two women went off and left Jack and Harley in the sitting room, where Harley proceeded to tell MacLaren what had happened with Beck.

"I don't know as I care to do it," Adair said, adjusting his headband.

"I've seen it before, Harley. Harald Beck wouldn't have got involved in this business two years ago. But he's got that damned black robe on now. And it's going to his head. By next year he'll figure himself sittin' to the right hand of God," MacLaren said, as much to himself as to Adair. "Guess he can't help himself. He's a damn lawyer. Lawyers and the law are like tent preachers and the Good Book. They get to readin' the words so close that the whole meaning of it goes right out the window."

"What ever it is, Beck's got it. I ain't never seen him carryin' on like that," Adair said, shaking his head from side to side. "Who the hell cares what McClintock does!"

"Way I heard it they ambushed the San Carlos runaways in the north end of the Hatchet Valley. That's U.S. Territory," MacLaren added.

"Hadn't struck me," Adair said. "I guess it is. But no doubt they were headed to join Victorio."

"There's more than one law that says that's murder," MacLaren added without any note of distress. "The law covers the Apaches, even when they're off the reservation."

"Guess, I was forgettin' they weren't down in Old Mexico," Adair said. "Wouldn't be murder in Old Mexico."

"Look, Harley," MacLaren said after he drained his glass, and came forward on his chair. "Don't go. To hell with it. It's not your fight really. Tell Beck to go fetch McClintock himself."

120

Adair's eyes brightened and a smile appeared. "Jack, you don't know how close I came to doing just that."

"This McClintock business isn't worth dying for," MacLaren said.

"I hadn't planned on dying," Adair came back.

"You mix it up with Jason McClintock and you'll be courting death. Jason McClintock is a hard man. There's no law that'll tame him and there's likely no jury west of the Mississippi that would convict him on any charge coming out of his killing Apaches after what happened to his family, and especially his daughter," MacLaren said with an air of certainty in his voice. "No, Harley, McClintock is fixed on killing Apaches in general and Victorio for certain. You fight McClintock and you'll have to kill him and the rest of his bunch."

"It'd be laugh on me to get hurt bringing him in only to have a jury set him free," Adair laughed.

"I guess it would. Besides you'd be pissin' in the wind. Dorsey Bowles, Jeb Hardin, and the rest won't ever be reined in by politicians, lawmen, and pompous men in black robes."

As MacLaren went on, Harley Adair was listening carefully. For one thing he had noticed that MacLaren hadn't said anything about Kriss Andersen, even though most of the newspaper accounts openly advertised the gangly, blond-headed young man as a full-fledged Indian fighter with several scalps on his belt.

"Look, Harley," MacLaren went on. "You know I've got no interest in preaching to another man. But I know what it's like wearing that gold star. First off, it's a god damned target. It's only by luck I'm sitting here today. You deal in the scum of the earth. Not one in ten of the men you hunt will ever fight you fair. Most will back-shoot you. I can count a half dozen times some hardcase tried to shoot me in the back. It's only by a twig being in the way, a sidewinder causing my horse to shy, and a bunch of other lucky events that kept me from taking a slug with my name on it. Christ's sakes I know you've heard that the outlaws have a price on your other ear. It's the talk of the Territory. All that for a wage that ought to be an insult to any man. A stablekeep makes more cleaning tack and shoveling horse shit!"

Harley Adair didn't take offense. He knew MacLaren had his best interests in mind. Ever since MacLaren had taken him under his wing, he'd begun to see life in a new light. He'd come to understand that folks pulled their britches and boots on the same way and that the only thing that held a man back from getting to greener pastures were the fences he built in his own mind. And it hadn't struck him lightly several weeks back when MacLaren offered to bring the him into the fold. MacLaren had only a few friends, and, after MacLaren's offer, he figured he was one of them.

"Hell, Harley," MacLaren said in a somber tone. "The best days of marshalin' are over anyhow. Folks are crowding into the territories. Squatting and farming. Building towns. And with them, all that follows. Whiskey merchants. Kitchenware drummers. Patent medicine peddlers. God damn people everywhere, all waiting at the door to come in now that the house is built and supper's on the table. Not a one of the fainthearts were here to lend a hand in the building. Lord knows the Marshal of the future will be handin' out peddlers permits, directing wagon traffic on main street, collecting taxes at gunpoint from the town's folks, and repossessing farms for the bankers. Imagine what it will be like once we get more preachers out here. The law will spend all it's time closing down whorehouses, saloons, and gambling parlors! And lockin' folks up for smoking loco weed!"

"Jack, this ain't Boston, Massachusetts!" Adair said, truly amused at MacLaren's diatribe.

"Well, hell. I'll say no more. Except that I insist you stay the night. Elaina will fry up a real feast."

"I'll buy that," Adair said.

"Just think on what I said, Harley. I've got more money that I do people I can trust to watch over it for me. I've been out and around talking up a cattleman's bank to some of the ranchers. Bill Finney needs a little competition for his bank. I could use a trusted man in that adventure."

"I will think on it, Jack," Adair said sincerely.

"You do that," MacLaren said, his demeanor suddenly serious and direct. "It hasn't slipped my mind that if you decide to head out after McClintock in the morning, you'll be going up against Kriss too. That'd be a sorry state of affairs."

"I guess it would," Adair said, reaching under his faded, blue denim vest and into his shirt pocket. "Take a look at this," he continued as he pulled out several neatly folded pieces of parchment. The top one was a warrant for the arrest of Kriss Andersen. The charge: premeditated murder.

24

While MacLaren and Harley Adair were jawing at the Sable Laire that Saturday morning, McClintock's men were saddling up.

Four days earlier, Dorsey Bowles and Chief White had returned to Columbus with the news that they had found the Apache stronghold in the Sierra el Tigre. McClintock had immediately begun to prepare his plan of attack, even though two of his five man search parties were still out.

In the past week, the camp had become a carnival, a fact which both bothered McClintock and pleased him. He knew that the local newspaper people, the photographers, and several crime writers from eastern police gazettes would all move public opinion to his favor. But he also knew that embellished versions of his escapades had already made the eastern papers. It wouldn't be long before he would feel the full weight of Governor Wallace and Judge Beck, now that the Hayes administration had again been embarrassed by the goings on in the New Mexico Territory. The papers were playing it up as the wholesale slaughter of placid reservation Indians.

When the last of his search parties had returned that very Saturday morning Adair had stopped by the Sable Laire, McClintock had immediately ordered the camp broken. McClintock wanted to be in Old Mexico by sundown.

Everyone was hurried as McClintock barked orders, and conveyed a sense of urgency. He'd chosen twenty-two men to go after Victorio and his renegades. The rest he was sending back to Albuquerque with the wagons and Jefferson Burn's mining engineer. McClintock had ordered every man to take only a bed roll, hard tack, jerky, and all the ammunition he could carry.

Kriss Andersen was being carried along by the events. He'd had serious reservations about the killing and the several days of celebration that followed. A little gremlin deep in his gut told him to get out while he still could. But being written up in the papers, having McClintock and the other men praise him for his decision to let the Apache kid go, and the constant telling of the story over and over again, had somehow pulled him deeper into McClintock's war. But none of that altered the fact that he was haunted by the face of defiant kid who'd faced his Winchester and, the desolate look in the eyes of the gut-shot Apache. Kriss couldn't get over the idea that the Apache he'd shot had been the boy's father. His dreams had been dominated by the skinny kid and the face of the dying Apache.

Kriss cursed himself for not having the courage to ride out of the camp and back to the Sable Laire, the place he'd started to call home only the week before he'd run off to kill Apaches. Shooting frogs in a pond, he thought to himself as he packed his saddle bags with food and cartridges. That wasn't how he'd imagined taking revenge for the murder of his parents and sisters. The ten Apaches they'd encountered in the Hatchet Valley were a sorry lot of humanity. And it bothered him plenty that the more gruesome characters in McClintock's bunch were getting worked up into a near frenzy over what they intended to do with the squaws they planned to capture. Bowles and Chief had reported several dozen women and children in the camp.

But Kriss Andersen's doubts were not enough to deter him. When McClintock and his twenty-two men filed out of their camp and headed south Kriss rode with the column.

* * * *

The blue-eyed Apache, Cain, watched their departure through a small, brass, U.S. Army issue telescope he'd taken from a Comanche he'd killed earlier in the summer. From a rock outcropping three quarters of a mile west of McClintock's camp, he'd been observing the white men for two days. Victorio and his warriors had been unaware of the fact that Dorsey Bowles and Chief White had discovered their camp in the Sierra el Tigre. But that was of no consequence. Victorio had broken camp the morning after the council and sent the women and children and several men west to another hideout he knew of in the eastern foothills of the Sierra Del Piñitos.

Once Victorio had made the decision to make war, he'd moved quickly to take the offensive. As a young man he'd listened carefully to the words of Mangas Coloradas. Mangas Coloradas had always insisted that when a war council had decided to fight, they must always take the offensive, use the elements of deception and surprise, and fight with superhuman ferocity once the battle had begun. The great Apache chief had always insisted that the decision to go to war should be made with great care. He'd held that avoiding a fight when the odds were against you, was a display of wisdom, not an act of cowardice. But Mangas Coloradas had insisted that, once the decision to spill blood had been made, there was no honor in anything but total devastation of the enemy.

Victorio had learned these lessons well.

25

McClintock's men moved at a steady pace all afternoon. The air was clear and crisp and the afternoon sun was invigorating. McClintock was determined to make camp west of Janos before sundown. He knew of an open valley which could be easily defended on all sides. Acutely aware that he was in enemy territory, he wanted to prevent the possibility of an ambush.

The men were engaged in their devil-may-care banter, each one working hard to keep the demons of doubt from his consciousness. Some used humor, some took solace in the perfect weather, and others like Dorsey Bowles whipped themselves up with talk about how they were going to blood the Indians and make use of their women.

Kriss Andersen was quiet that Saturday afternoon, lost in a jumble of disconnected thoughts, trying to make sense of nonsense. He rode as far away from Bowles as possible, partly to avoid the man's stink, but mostly to avoid his talk.

McClintock and his twenty-two riders made their camp site by late afternoon. McClintock immediately ordered five men to scout the perimeter of the open valley, looking for any signs of Apaches. McClintock was a cautious man with many years of schooling in the ways of the Apache. And he sensed that his men were not taking the threat seriously.

"You men who are going to ride the perimeter! Keep your damned eyes open!" McClintock shouted as his horse danced about in the middle of the activity. "Victorio ain't no wore out, half starved reservation jumper like the ones you shot down in the Hatchet Valley."

McClintock knew that Victorio was in the league with Geronimo, Cochise, and Mangas Coloradas. And he had little doubt that the chief had a network of informers across the southern sections of the

126

Arizona and New Mexico Territories and in Old Mexico. In fact, he'd had the feeling that they were being watched most of the afternoon. He had no sign of it, but where Apaches were involved, McClintock had a sixth sense which rarely failed him.

"While those boys are riding the perimeter of the camp, I want five other men on foot posted at the edge of the camp," McClintock ordered, still mounted, and squinting into the late afternoon sun. "You over there," he said to one of his men, pointing toward a small rise in the open, due east of the camp. "You. Stand fifty yards yonder and keep an eye on that tree line," he shouted, waiving his weathered hand as he maneuvered his horse, surveying the landscape.

For another hour, Jason McClintock tended to such details, never quite satisfied that things were right. Though Bowles hadn't counted many warriors in the Apache camp in the Sierra el Tigre, his description of the camp and the number of wickiups led McClintock to believe that Victorio had a bigger band of bucks than he had at first imagined possible.

With the sun finally behind the mountains, McClintock ordered the small campfires killed. "And keep your makin's in your pockets. Strike a match out here or draw on a cigarette and you can see it for miles," he ordered with all the authority of a seasoned company commander. "We'll change the watch at two o'clock. I'll oversee the current watch. Bowles will have the next watch. And keep the corks in your jugs; this is Apache territory!" he continued as he walked about the camp.

McClintock stopped and made eye contact with every man in the camp. "One more thing. Don't let me catch a man sleeping on watch. I'll shoot his ass sure as the sunrise and Bowles has orders to do the same!"

There wasn't any grumbling, but the camp had taken on an air of a military bivouac. Many of McClintock's men had served in the army, some in General Lee's army, some in Grant's. But there wasn't a one who cared for the life. So McClintock's orders didn't go down easily.

The cool night unfolded quietly. There wasn't a whisp of a breeze. There was no moon, but the clear sky was a sea of starlight.

The watch changed without incident at two o'clock. The men who'd come off the picket were cold and tired. Kriss had been one of the outriders, so he and the others who had been mounted tended to their horses, tack, and bedrolls. Assured that all was quiet, Kriss fell quickly off to sleep once the warmth of the bedroll eased the cold in his body and the stars eased the cold in his soul.

Except for the hoot of a single nearby owl, and the howl of a distant pack of wolves, the night had continued to be quiet. Jeb Hardin had kept pacing back and forth all night to ease the chill and fight off the temptation to rest his eyes. He'd cursed his watch more than once. He hated being on foot. Hardin felt stark naked without a horse under him. So when the gray sky began to roll in from the east, he felt better.

A half hour later when the very first warming rays of the sun hit his face he heaved a sigh of relief.

He had no sooner exhaled his sigh when he suddenly felt a bump from behind. Before he could comprehend what was happening his legs weakened and he went to his knees. Then he felt a burning in his throat as something pulled him backward. When he saw the Apache over him he tried to shout a warning but he couldn't make any sound. He looked down and saw his right leg spring out from underneath his body and noticed it kicking out and flopping side to side. It didn't feel like his leg. And blood. Blood everywhere. Blood squirting. He looked up into the mean, dark eyes of Ciervo Blanco who was kneeling behind him. The Apache smiled at him and Jeb Hardin died, his throat cut clear through to his spine.

Like Ciervo Blanco, other warriors had squirmed out of their hiding places where they had secreted themselves before McClintock had made camp. Some were hidden under scrub growth, others had buried themselves in the ground, a favorite Apache ruse.

Like Jeb Hardin, the other four walking picket had died quickly and quietly. Five men were still up on horseback, but as soon as Ciervo Blanco gave his shrill war cry, two of the riders were jumped, pulled from their horses, and killed. Two others instinctively kicked their horses toward the camp. One hundred mounted Apaches dressed and painted to die in battle, surged from the very tree line which had earlier concerned McClintock.

Dorsey Bowles saw them coming, turned, and kicked his horse toward the camp which was only three thousand feet dead ahead. Bowles saw two other riders side by side, headed toward the camp. But just as they reached the camp perimeter where Jeb Hardin should have been, an Apache stood up and leveled his Winchester on the riders. Bowles saw both riders shot methodically from their saddles. No fool, Bowles knew it was going to be a one sided battle. He reined his horse ninety degrees from the camp and abandoned his fellow militiamen. He had a strong horse and he intended to run until it dropped. Several quick glances over his shoulder revealed three mounted Apaches on his tail. He hadn't gone a hundred feet when he started hearing the whine of rifle slugs followed closely by the reports of the rifles aimed at his back. Then his luck ran off and left him. He took a slug high in the right shoulder. The blow nearly knocked him from his horse. He feet came out of the stirrups and he slipped halfway off his galloping gelding. Instinctively, he grabbed a handful of mane with his right hand and the saddle horn with his left. He fought his way back into the saddle, knowing exactly what kind of death would await him if he fell.

With no first or second line of defense, Victorio, decked out in full war regalia, led his men toward the camp. The rifle fire had awakened the sleeping men. But by the time they'd untangled themselves from their blankets, ninety warriors were on top of them. The sound of rifle fire was deafening. Kriss jumped out of his blankets and stood barefooted and dumbfounded, looking at Apaches everywhere, reining their ponies, shooting rifles and pistols at the men still on the ground, and hooting and screaming oaths. He saw one Apache take a man's arm off with a huge machete.

Jason McClintock pulled his pistol but didn't get off a shot before an Apache ran over him with his stocky pony. Once McClintock went down, the Apache urged his pony to dance on McClintock's back as the leader of the doomed group tried to fend off the horse's hooves.

Then Kriss gathered his wits, saw an opening, and ran on pure animal instinct, leaving behind the gory slaughter. For the best part of a minute it looked like Kriss had escaped the deadly chaos. Then he heard ponies coming up on him from behind. Once they sounded close enough, he stopped, turned, and went for his pistol. As the Apaches were only fifty feet away Kriss Andersen clawed at his side for the Colt that was still back in his bedroll.

Suddenly aware of his impending death, he squared off to jump at one of the Indians as they went by. He wasn't going to go out easy. It was then that he saw the scrawny Apache who'd defied him and his Winchester in the Hatchet Valley. The skinny Apache had blood in his eyes.

The Indians pulled up their horses and circled Kriss, mocking him. The skinny Apache was shouting something in broken English about his father. The other swung a war club over his head in a large circle. Tethered to his wrist by a three foot leather thong, the club was a two foot long oak handle with an egg-shaped stone lashed to it.

In an instant of furious anger, Kriss lurched at the kid, pulling him from his pony.

That's when the other Apache moved in and caught Kriss Andersen square in the side of skull with the deadly stone head of the weapon which had been speeding around the perimeter of a five foot circle.

Kriss Andersen went down quick and hard.

26

At Jack MacLaren's insistence, Harley Adair had stayed on at the Sable Laire. Sunday had been a lazy day under more crystal clear skies, a day filled with laughter, good food from Elaina's kitchen, and ample wine and whiskey.

Harley, Mary Beth, and MacLaren had nothing to say about Judge Beck, Kriss Andersen, or Victorio and his renegades. But that didn't mean that the problem wasn't tucked away in the back of their heads, and gnawing away at their innards. MacLaren had barely slept on Saturday night. Sunday night his mind continued to go 'round and 'round on Kriss Andersen while Mary Beth tossed and turned at his side. Harley laid up half the night staring out the window at the new moon, still unsure of what trail he'd take when he left the Sable Laire in the morning.

Mary Beth had been acutely aware of MacLaren's concerns, but she'd known MacLaren long enough to know when he was in no mood to hear from her. It was obvious he was keeping his own council on the matter and that her opinions would not be welcome.

Monday morning at breakfast, they continued their good natured give and take, adding Elaina to the exchanges. But there was still no mention of the events which most occupied their minds.

That changed suddenly when Billy Wilcomb, MacLaren's partner in the William Bell Hotel, arrived at the Sable Laire, his horse lathered up from the hard ride.

One of the hands took Wilcomb's horse and Joe Harper lead Wilcomb to the house. The commotion had brought MacLaren, Adair, and Mary Beth from their seats at the breakfast table to the ranch house veranda where they met Wilcomb and Joe Harper.

Wilcomb pulled a folded copy of the Las Vegas News from his hip pocket and unfurled the eight-page news sheet, revealing the bold headline: McClintock Slaughtered At Janos. And in smaller type below: Victorio's Renegades Rout Citizen Militia.

Before any of the trio on the veranda could speak, Billy Wilcomb rattled on. "There's not much more in the story. Nobody knows much yet. Only that Dorsey Bowles looks to be the only one who got out with his hide. He's wounded and bein' tended to in Las Cruces. The story says Bowles figures everyone's dead unless some were carried off to provide the reds with their devilish amusements. Paper says Victorio had a hundred warriors that came out of nowhere."

MacLaren snatched the paper from Wilcomb and began to read.

"What else did you hear, Billy?" Adair asked. "The Mexicans on Victorio's trail?"

"Ain't heard of it. Hell, every man in Diáz' army leaks his pants at the mention of Victorio."

"When?" Adair asked.

"Yesterday morning," MacLaren answered, his head still buried in the newspaper.

"I stopped by the News on the way out here and old Clement showed me the telegraph he used to write the story," Wilcomb added. "Wasn't but five lines saying what I've already told."

Harley and Mary Beth glanced at each other and then looked at MacLaren who was still reading. Both had the same thought. If Kriss Andersen was dead at the hands of Victorio, MacLaren wouldn't be fit company for a month of Sundays.

MacLaren raised his eyes from the news sheet and said simply: "I'm goin' to Las Cruces."

"I'm comin' with you," Joe Harper chimed in.

"No, Joe. I need you here. Besides, I'm not goin' to fight. I'm just goin' to see what happened. If the kid's dead, I want to bring him back to be laid out with his folks. If he isn't dead I want to find him."

"Well I'm goin' for sure," Adair said.

"I'd welcome it, Harley," MacLaren said sincerely. "That tin star of yours might do us some good."

"I'll tack up the horses," Harper said as he turned and headed for the stable.

"Saddle our horses, Joe. And put good halters on Airborne and Muffin. We'll be traveling light and fast so we'll want the two extra horses with us. And break out two extra sets of hobbles."

Harper raised his hand to answer, not breaking his stride.

Adair fell in behind Harper, anxious to tend to his own gear, and Wilcomb followed to tend to his overheated horse.

MacLaren went back into the house, Mary Beth close on his heels.

Once inside, MacLaren noticed Elaina standing off to the side daubing tears from the corners of her eyes with a dish towel. The full impact of the news finally hit him and Elaina's tears brought a painful lump to his throat.

"Now Elaina, we don't know enough to get all wrought up," MacLaren said after a moment's pause to gain his composure. "That's why I'm headed to Las Cruces. Damn newspapers are as unreliable as a parson's wife."

Elaina smiled. "Señor Jack," she scolded.

"Well, they write up a heavy rain to sound like the Great Flood. Now get some food together for Harley and me. We've got a long ride to Las Cruces."

Elaina went to her kitchen and immediately went to her task.

"Jack," Mary Beth said, uttering her first word since they'd jumped up from the breakfast table. "Why don't you wait a day or two? No need to run off half cocked. The telegraph will be full of details all week. Clement's paper will be nothing but."

"I'm goin'," he grunted as he headed for the bedroom.

"Well then!" she said angrily and loudly as he stomped to the bedroom. "You stay away from those god damned red savages, Jack MacLaren!"

27

MacLaren and Adair had ridden steadily for two days, sleeping only briefly the first night. The clear weather had continued and the new moon had slain the darkness.

Both men were dog tired and as they topped the ridge just east of Las Cruces and saw the dim lights of the town in the distance.

MacLaren hauled in his horse without a word to Adair and the two men stopped to survey the horizon. Then, without so much as a grunt, MacLaren kicked his horse into a strong trot, obviously invigorated by the sight of the town. Adair wheezed a sigh of frustration, lifted and reseated his Stetson, and followed MacLaren's impulsive lead, the two spare mounts in tow.

Familiar with Las Cruces, MacLaren rode straight for the south side of the town. He was headed for the Tres Hermanas Saloon on Calle Centro. The Tres Hermanas had been the center of all night time activity in Las Cruces ever since the end of the war. Started by three whores in 1864, the rambling wooden structure had a reputation among grifters, gamblers, hold-up artists, and hired guns. Though not a pretty building, the sturdy saloon served as the headquarters for half the hardcases in New Mexico and Arizona.

MacLaren figured that Dorsey Bowles would be there if he hadn't already died and gone to sit with the Devil.

As the pair of worn and soiled riders approached the saloon, the noise coming from the place filled the street. The sun had been down for two hours and the Tres Hermanas was alive with raucous laughter, loud piano music which betrayed the player's drunken state, and the din of fifty booze-animated conversations.

MacLaren rode up to the hitching rail two buildings south of the saloon, dismounted, and secured his reins. In one motion he hauled his stubby .12 gauge from its soft cowhide saddle sheath and headed toward the noise. Harley Adair quickly dismounted and secured his horse and the two he had in trail.

"Hold on Jack," Adair said from behind as he mounted the plankwalk which ran the length of the street, his voice tired and plaintive. "What the hell are you headed in there for?" he asked.

"No better place in the territory to find out what went on down Janos way than in this den of thieves!" MacLaren answered, his stride unbroken by Adair's question.

MacLaren pushed through the batwing doors and stopped six feet inside the saloon to look around. There were the usual scofflaws and an unusual number of drunken uniformed U.S. Cavalry Troopers. Not seeing Bowles, MacLaren headed for the bar as Adair stepped through the saloon doors. When MacLaren demanded a beer, the noise subsided. In five seconds, the place was quiet. Even the piano player had stopped.

MacLaren turned and saw the youthful Harley Adair just inside the door. Adair had his almond-colored Montana Peak Stetson square in place. His black headband, embroidered with the outline of connecting red diamonds, swept down over his earhole, and his shiny gold star shone as bright as the noonday sun. Somehow the sight of his friend struck him funny and a toothy smile spread across his weathered face. Harley Adair, now twenty-five years old, had only been a U.S. Marshal for a year, and with his presence he could make a saloon as quiet as a funeral service.

Adair, suddenly aware of the effect the star had had on the party, struck a pose, and then strode toward MacLaren and demanded a beer still two paces from the long, thick rough-sawn oak bar.

MacLaren took a long pull on his beer, never allowing his hand to stray too far from his stubby .12 gauge resting on the bar. After Adair had had a sip of beer, the piano player picked up where he'd left off and some talk resumed. But most eyes were still on Adair, reminding MacLaren of what it had been like to walk around with a target on your chest. It didn't escape MacLaren or Adair that a half a dozen men abandoned their whores and card games and quietly slinked out the front door.

"Better go after 'em, Harley," MacLaren said quietly with his grin still in place. "Likely a poster on 'em somewhere."

"I ain't in the mood," Adair said as he drained half his glass in one swallow.

MacLaren finished his beer while keeping his eyes fixed on Adair's eyes, the message in the stare obvious. The Tres Hermanas was enemy territory. Watch your back!

"Another one?" the burly barkeep asked MacLaren.

"Fill it up," MacLaren answered. "And I'd appreciate knowing the latest tales on what happened down near Janos Sunday past."

"God damned slaughter's what happened," the bartender said as he pumped Adair's beer, obviously hot to tell the story again. "Dorsey Bowles is the only one that got away and he's laid up with a bum wing."

"Everyone else killed?" MacLaren asked.

"Ain't heard. Mexican soldiers gathered up what was left and hauled the dead to the border. Why the hell they didn't plant 'em down Old Mexico I can't figure," the barkeep grunted, shaking his head in disgust. "Army's worked all day saltin' and wrappin' 'em over to their camp on the river."

"Who's wantin' to know about McClintock's men?" someone asked from several places down the bar.

MacLaren and Adair turned to face two Army troopers who were obviously lost in the jug. Both soldiers were small and wiry, and looked as if they'd ridden a tornado into the Tres Hermanas. The Sergeant had a large scar on his cheek and the corporal obviously had African slave in his blood a ways back.

"Harley Adair is askin'. U.S. Marshal."

The two troopers moved up the bar, looking down at Harley's badge and then at each other.

"You with the detail tending to the bodies?" MacLaren asked directly.

"Yes, sir!" the corporal said.

"How many of McClintock's men do you have," MacLaren asked.

"What was it Henry?" the sergeant asked the corporal. "Nineteen?"

"It was," the corporal answered.

"Were you fixin' the bodies today?" Adair asked.

"Yes, sir, Marshal," the corporal answered. "And that's why we're standing here drunk as reservation Indians. And I might jest stay drunk for the rest of my life 'cause o' what I seen today."

"You know how many went down to Janos with McClintock's bunch?" MacLaren asked the Sergeant.

"Got no notion of that, mister. You'll have to ask Bowles. He's right yonder," the scarface sergeant mumbled, pointing up toward the end of the row of doors which ran the length of the second floor landing. "Hold up with a two dollar whore and a bottle of whiskey, tendin' to a leakin' shoulder."

"In those dead you got out at your camp. Was there a blond

136

headed kid? Long blond hair, damn near white? Skinny? About six feet?" Adair asked calmly and directly.

The two horse soldiers looked at each other and giggled like two kids struck funny by an old lady falling in a muddy street.

"Answer the man," MacLaren growled at the troopers, his eyes filled with enough sudden anger to momentarily sober the pair up.

"Don't get your dander up, Mister," The corporal said. "But the marshal askin' about hair. Those boys out to the camp ain't got no hair. And that ain't all they ain't got."

"Apaches don't usually take scalps," MacLaren shot back.

"Ceptin' mebbe one for a scalp dance," the corporal chimed in.

"Well they took these, Mister," the sergeant said, his voice becoming loud, and his demeanor threatening. "And they cut them boys up so bad you can't tell what's what, never mind who's who."

The talk of the trooper had once again caused the saloon to go silent. The piano player quit, got up and went for whiskey.

MacLaren was quickly overcome with a sense of despair. He figured Kriss Andersen for dead. And he was sure Victorio and Nana would soon follow the kid to the grave. Apaches usually only took one scalp when they took any at all. And that was for a scalp dance in the river to purify their weapons after battle. Mass scalping and other forms of mutilation of the dead were sure signs that Victorio's people had gone mad with revenge and obviously had no notion of ever leaving the world peacefully. He'd always held out a slim chance that there'd be some way Victorio might return to make a new agreement with the government as he'd done several times before. But MacLaren knew that Victorio would be hounded to his grave after the massacre of McClintock's men. It all seemed so damned senseless.

Despair quickly turning to anger, MacLaren snatched his .12 gauge off the bar, pushed his way between the two soldiers and headed for the stairs. After climbing the stairs two at a time, he reached the landing and pushed open the first door only to find a whore at work on her customer. Not finding Bowles, he opened the second door to find a horse soldier and a whore pulling their clothes on. Behind the third door he found what he was looking for.

"Bowles, I want a word with you," MacLaren said, ignoring the woman sitting in the chair clad only in a skimpy silk nightie. "I want to know what the hell happened in Janos. How the hell did that happen?"

"Well, hello Jack MacLaren. Come right in. Make yourself to home!" Bowles answered, his face screwed up with displeasure.

"All right Bowles. Just talk to me and I'll leave you to your girl-friend here. I had friends in that bunch. I want to know what the hell happened to them."

Bowles hoisted himself up on his pillow with his good arm. The sheet fell away revealing a bandage red with leaking blood. He snatched his bottle, took a pull and held it our toward MacLaren, smiling, revealing teeth that looked like a row of black pegs.

MacLaren begged off the bottle with a nod.

"Why hell, Jack. Wasn't much to it. They must have took a chance we'd camp there and hid themselves around Apache-style be-fore we got there. When the time come, they took out our sentries and then a hundred of the red devils come on us like a flash of lightning. I jest run after I was hit. Shooting didn't last but two or three minutes. Most of the boys was likely shot in their bedrolls. Couple of 'em set out after me and I took a slug right away. But I had the best damn horse in the world under me. Old Starduster got a good lead on 'em for me. I saw a good place for an ambush. I jumped off, waited a half a minute, and sent both the red bastards straight to hell. One shot each," he added proudly. "I took their hair and their ponies and made straight for the border."

"You see the kid, Kriss Andersen?"

"The white-haired kid." Bowles replied.

"Yeah," MacLaren said.

"Didn't see nothin' Jack," Bowles said hoisting his whiskey bottle again. "They jest come out of the dawn light like a passel of mad ghosts. Happened so fast it ain't clear in my mind yet."

Bowles took a long draw on his whiskey bottle and the whore rearranged herself so MacLaren could get peek at what she had for sale.

"How many of you were there?" MacLaren asked as Adair ap-peared in the doorway.

"Twenty-two and Jason, the poor son of a bitch."

"Take out Bowles here and that has the Army coming up three short," Adair said as he came along side of MacLaren.

MacLaren lifted his black, flat-brim Stetson, raked his fingers through his sandy hair, and replaced his hat. His one and only thought at that moment was that he was tired.

Bowles took another large swallow from his bottle of cheap whis-key. MacLaren's eyes made contact with the woman in the room and he turned to look at her.

"You want a closer look-see, mister?" she said as she got up.

MacLaren's face became a red mask of disgust. He spun on his heel, brushed past Harley Adair and stomped out of the room muttering to himself as Bowles scolded his whore for working on new business while he still had time on the clock.

28

MacLaren stomped through the crowd in the Tres Hermanas and broke through the batwing doors into the crisp night air. "Whores, outlaws, politicians, preachers, and drummers," he mumbled to himself as he took in the fresh night air. "Kick and scratch yourself through life. Banging up against the god damned rabble every day of your time. For what?" he said to the stars. "You suffer through it and then the god damned worms eat you."

"What?" Adair asked from behind, his chiseled features twisted into a mask of frustration.

"You know, Harley, it's a good god damned thing a man doesn't know much when he's your age. If he did, he wouldn't get out of friggin' bed in the morning. It'd be too much for too many years."

With that, MacLaren lurched off down the boardwalk toward his horse. MacLaren felt as empty as a ghost town save the nagging image of a dead Kriss Andersen.

MacLaren sheathed his .12 gauge, mounted up and made for the Army camp on the eastern shore of the Rio Grande. Adair stood for a minute wondering if MacLaren hadn't lost his senses. Then he mounted up and, followed on with the spare horses, wondering what the hell MacLaren had meant about not getting out of bed in the morning. "The man don't make sense sometimes," he mumbled to himself as he slowly made his way toward the Army bivouac.

MacLaren dismounted at the temporary Army camp and sought out the commanding officer. A sentry pointed to a well lit tent a hundred feet toward the river. As he walked toward the tent, he saw cheap pine caskets piled up, six across and three high, with a lone casket on top. He hadn't seen anything like it since the war.

"Hello in there," MacLaren said, rubbing the two day growth on his chin.

Lieutenant Zeke Morrow pushed aside the tent flap and stepped into the night air.

"Jack MacLaren," Morrow said as he extended a hand. "What brings you down here?"

"Howdy, Zeke," MacLaren said, pleased that the detail commander was someone he knew. "I guess that pile of boxes yonder brings me to Las Cruces. One of my men ran off to join up with McClintock. A kid really," MacLaren added, his voice revealing that the kid was more than a hired hand.

Adair appeared, finally catching up with MacLaren.

"Lieutenant," Adair said, leaning forward in his saddle, tipping his hat.

"Marshal," Morrow replied. "I got word you were supposed to be here several days back with a handful of warrants."

"I reckon there's no longer any need for warrants," Adair said.

"You know each other?" MacLaren interrupted.

"We've worked together on several occasions," Morrow said. Then he shouted to a trooper near by, "Corporal Skinner! Get a couple of men to tend to our visitors' horses!" Morrow turned back toward MacLaren and insisted they spend the night. "Come on in, boys," Morrow said. "I've got a bottle of grade A Kentucky bourbon inside. And maybe I can settle up this business of your hired hand."

MacLaren and Adair followed and took Morrow up on his offer. After a tin cup full of the smooth liquor, MacLaren felt more at ease. But his lack of sleep was catching up with him so he got to the point.

"Do you know who you've got boxed up out there?" MacLaren asked Morrow.

"We know eleven certain and we've got a description on the other eight, some detailed, some not so detailed. Victorio and his people chopped 'em up and Mother Nature didn't do 'em any good."

"Kriss Andersen," MacLaren said immediately, moving up to the edge of his stool. "Just under six feet? Long blond hair? Just seventeen years old. Skinny as a shovel handle."

Morrow looked up at MacLaren. "I gather the boy was more than a hired hand," he said, his voice striking a somber note when he saw the pain in Jack MacLaren's tired eyes. "The boy kin to you?"

"No," MacLaren said, staring into the amber liquid in his coffee cup. "A friend is all."

"He's the kid I was tellin' you about, Zeke, when you and me were running down the Buchanan brothers in late July," Adair added.

"Remember? The kid's the reason Burleigh Simmons and his boys got cheated out of the rest of my ears and the rest of Jack's fingers."

Morrow nodded understanding, glancing at MacLaren's hand as he reached for a sheath of papers on the small, fold-up camp table next to his cot. He'd remembered the story because of Adair's ear.

MacLaren and Adair sipped the last of their bourbon while Morrow thumbed through the papers, stopping to read the handwriting on each sheet.

Then he looked up into MacLaren's bloodshot eyes. "The boy's not among the identified and I'm pretty certain that he fits none of the descriptions I've got on the no-names."

"You can't be sure?" MacLaren asked.

"No, I can't. But the eight descriptions I've got here all have something that seems to rule out the kid," the Lieutenant said, handing the sheets of paper to MacLaren. "Here, look for yourself."

Adair and Morrow made small talk while MacLaren studied the papers like a lawyer reading a contract.

"We figure Jason McClintock's not here either," the Calvary officer said when MacLaren looked up from the papers. "If the Apaches have him, they'll take two weeks to kill him. That old son-of-a-bitch will die harder than he ever lived," Morrow said, shaking his head slowly.

Jack MacLaren popped up from his stool, laid the papers on the table, offered the army officer a cursory thanks and ducked out of the tent flap, all in one fluid motion. Adair looked at Morrow and they both shrugged at his sudden departure.

"He ain't been right since the kid ran off," Adair said to Morrow. "He's taken a shine to the kid. You'd think he's the kid's pappy the way he's carrin' on."

"Damn sorry to hear it. I never figured this Victorio business would fall this way. MacLaren's friendly with the Chief isn't he?," Morrow said, stroking his black, handlebar mustache. "Thought sure McClintock and his boys would kill those renegades and save us the trouble."

"What little talk I've heard from Jack, Victorio ain't a pushover," Adair answered as he stepped toward the tent opening. "Might keep that in mind if you go against Victorio and that son of his, Nana."

"You can count on it, Harley. But I'm hoping to avoid it. I just got a telegraph today from Colonel Harper in Santa Fe. President Hayes is putting heavy pressure on President Díaz. Hayes wants the Mexican Army to hunt down Victorio and kill him."

"Hell, those boys in Diáz Army would shit their britches at the sight of Victorio. It'll take the U.S. Army to do the job," Adair said as he ducked out of the tent. "So long Zeke, and thanks for the drink."

Adair paused and looked into the darkness. He saw MacLaren headed toward the horses and the soldiers tending them, so he struck up a jog to keep pace.

"I'm headed for Janos," MacLaren said to Adair as the Marshal arrived at his side.

"Tonight! Are you crazy?"

"First light," MacLaren said. "I don't believe the kid's in one of those boxes. I aim to find out what happened to him. We'll camp here by the river tonight."

"What do you figure we'll find in Janos?" Adair asked as they began to lead the horses toward a stand of cotton woods next to the river.

"If I can find him, I know of a man who will be able to answer a few questions."

"You think we'll be able to find him?" Adair asked.

"We'll find nothing. You're going north to set about your own business. There's no use for a U.S. Marshal down in Old Mexico."

29

Jack MacLaren lay awake in his bedroll. Though dog tired, he couldn't sleep. The events of recent days ran helter skelter through his head. To compound the problem, part of the reason he couldn't sleep was his being upset that he couldn't sleep. There hadn't been two dozen nights in the last twenty years when sleep had evaded him. And he couldn't help note that half of those sleepless nights had visited him since his first encounter with Kriss Andersen. MacLaren had always said that "a man who can't sleep is a man fighting his nature. And a man who fights his nature is a damn fool."

Since three full days had passed since Victorio's raid on McClintock's militia, MacLaren knew that the odds dictated that the missing trio were either dead or headed out of harm's way. He knew they were most likely dead. But he held out a sliver of hope that they might be hiding out until the U.S. Government had had time to forget about the whole thing. Victorio had stirred up a storm that had made its way all the way to Washington and unleashed its thunder and lightning over the nation's Capitol. Every soul in the Territories knew that every man in McClintock's militia had a federal murder charge on his head.

All that aside, Jack MacLaren knew what bothered him most. He was disobeying his instincts again. His ride across the Territory in pursuit of Kriss Andersen went against his highly developed ideas about a man's business here on this earth. And as he lay under the new moon listening to the soothing sounds of the Rio Grande clash with the snoring of Harley Adair, he reminded himself again that a man's primary business was to mind his own damn business! And that the only time another man's business became his business was when that other man set out to harm him with fraud or violence. He knew his riding around the countryside poking his nose into the affairs of other folks was a prescription for trouble. He felt it in his bones. He knew that he ought to saddle up in the morning and return to the Sable Laire. The last time he'd fought his instincts and agreed to help his friend Judge Beck, Burleigh Simmons had come within a whisker of killing him.

Victorio had taken his path, and Kriss Andersen had plotted his own course. That was unalterable reality.

But MacLaren couldn't kick Kriss Andersen from his mind. Images of the kid kept walking through his skull. Kriss stubbornly, although amateurishly, trying to break a wild stallion. The kid fiddling with his collection of guns and rifles. Kriss cutting up out on the range with the ranch hands. Kriss laughing at Joe Harper's stories about the ladies he'd known. Kriss blushing when Harper provided some of the lurid details of his encounters. And always the image of Kriss Andersen sitting up under that canvas lean-to, a blank look on his face, his still-smoking .45 Colt in his hand. To MacLaren's way of thinking that episode had been one of the two strangest episodes in his life, the other being his wake-up in a Lacy Springs farmhouse during the war. And he could never get over the fact that he and the kid had rifle slug scars across their skulls in exactly the same spot.

A kid, nine-tenths, dead, coming to life at that very moment and saving his life with three perfectly placed shots was more than he could explain with reason.

His disjointed thoughts rattled around in his mind for a while longer until total fatigue won out. As he was falling off, he thought of all the things he wanted to do before winter set in, his cattleman's bank at the top of the list. That was all it took for his troubled mind to succumb to his tired body. Jack MacLaren soon fell into a deep sleep, his plans for the morning in limbo.

30

Early Wednesday evening MacLaren dismounted, unsheathed his twelve gauge, and squinted up at a crudely painted sign which said, in peeling white letters on a sun-bleached blue background: CANTINA. He looped his reins around the hitching post and walked through the opening under the sign.

He saw at once who he was looking for. The man always stood out in a crowd. His stubby shotgun in hand, both hammers cocked, he walked up to the notorious half-breed. He was dressed in an Apache buckskin shirt adorned with colorful beadwork, the pants of a Mexican soldier, and the boots of a U.S. Cavalryman decked out with gaudy silver spurs that had never been cleaned since he'd killed the man who used to own them. A large sombrero put the crowning touch on his strange get-up. Oddly though, any man who looked at the Apache usually looked beyond the outlandish costume and focused on the piercing blue eyes which shot out from under the sombrero or the oversized machete which hung from his side.

MacLaren walked toward the half-breed Apache, making eye contact before he was halfway across the dirt floor.

"Jack MacLaren," the breed said with only the slightest Mexican accent. "What brings you to old Mexico?"

"Cain," MacLaren said greeting the Apache. "Cervesa," MacLaren added as he reached the bar and looked momentarily toward the señorita behind the bar.

"Dos," Cain added, holding up two fingers.

"Cain, I haven't got time to screw around and drink beer with you," MacLaren said just as Adair stepped into the doorless opening and leaned against one of the posts which framed the door in the adobe building. "That fight with McClintock on Sunday couldn't have come to pass without you being in the thick of it."

The few quiet conversations in the bar ceased immediately.

"Bad day for the gringo McClintock," Cain said, his voice revealing his joy. "But I know nothing of it."

"Horse shit, Cain," MacLaren growled. "Now you and me have known each other for the better part of the past ten years. You know I've got no ax to grind with the Apache. You know Victorio and his bunch have always been welcome on my land and free to slaughter my beef when food is short."

"I know this," Cain said, appearing bored with MacLaren.

"Well then!" MacLaren went on, his face reddening, his voice becoming more demanding. "I want to know if you've got any prisoners from your fight with McClintock."

The blue-eyed Apache swallowed a third of his glass of beer and turned to face MacLaren with a blank stare. He said nothing.

"Best I can tell there was a blond-headed kid with McClintock on Sunday. The boy ran off and joined McClintock to avenge the death of his family. I figure it was you and the others who killed his people up around Mineral Hill the day after you busted out of Fort Sumner.

Cain sipped his beer, keeping his eyes focused on MacLaren.

MacLaren thought he saw a knowing look flash across the half breed's face.

Cain had remembered the family. He understood there was a coiled rattlesnake next to him. He knew that MacLaren was not a man to be taken lightly. He also knew he would like to kill the white man. Cain hated all white men, all Mexicans, and most Indians. But Cain knew that the Apache who killed or harmed Jack MacLaren without cause would answer personally to Victorio and Nana.

"Well? Speak up, Cain," MacLaren demanded. "I've got no time or desire for idle talk."

"It is not my place to speak, MacLaren," Cain said, unwilling to hide his disdain for the former lawman. "You know the ways of the Apache."

"Is the kid your prisoner?" MacLaren demanded.

Cain offered no answer.

"Take me to Victorio's camp," MacLaren demanded, knowing that Cain would never break the Apache code of silence on a matter like this.

"You, but not him," Cain said directly, pointing to Adair.

"We both go," MacLaren said. It was not a matter for debate.

* * * *

The sun was gone, leaving only an orange glow on the western horizon when the half-breed, MacLaren, and Adair rode out of Janos. MacLaren's strength for the all-night ride ahead had been restored by a large plate of rice smothered with chile con pollo and the prospect of learning something more about Kriss Andersen.

There was little talk as they moved on at a steady lope, single file down roads and animal trails. Cain knew every inch of the land, frequently leaving the main wagon roads to take a shortcut across a wash or to go over a hill rather than around it.

MacLaren's conflict over returning to the Sable Laire or pushing on to find out what happened to the kid had been resolved. Earlier that morning when he and Adair had arisen at Lieutenant Zeke Morrow's bivouac on the Rio Grande he'd gotten another good look at the nineteen stacked caskets. It was at that moment he'd decided to determine the fate of Kriss Andersen and put his mind at ease. For the first time since he'd known Mary Beth, he'd understood how it must hurt her to have never known the fate of her daughters.

Though MacLaren had insisted that Harley Adair stay put, Adair was set on riding with MacLaren. When MacLaren had reminded him that he was still a duly sworn Territorial Marshal, Harley had simply scratched a two line letter of resignation and handed the letter, the warrants, and the star to Zeke Morrow. Adair had insisted that the fate of Kriss Andersen was as much his business as it was the business of Jack MacLaren.

The pace set by the half-breed Cain on his muscled pinto stallion kept MacLaren and Adair working their horses harder than they should have, but they weren't about to ask the Apache to back off. MacLaren hadn't ridden that far, or that hard for a dozen years. His legs and his back ached and his lack of sleep left his mind dull. Had it not been for the clear weather and the sliver of new moon, the night ride would have been a hellish business.

As they rode twenty miles up a dry wash toward San Lazaro, the sun came up and began to warm their backs. It had finally become too much for MacLaren, and he spurred his horse forward and pulled up along side the Apache.

"Cain," MacLaren said. "Where the hell are we headed? California?"

The blue-eyed Apache smiled at MacLaren. The Indian didn't look like he'd been in the saddle for eight minutes, let alone eight hours.

"We're going to have to pull up and rest the horses," MacLaren said. "I'm not going to ruin a good horse for any damn reason."

"One hour, MacLaren," the breed grunted, his pace unaltered. "We keep riding."

Just west of San Lazaro, they left the wash and headed into the Sierra Del Piñitos. The trio walked slowly up the foot hills with the two spare horses in trail. Cain led them through a series of passes and along natural trails carved in the sides of the foothills.

"Up to your left, Harley," MacLaren said. "We've got company."

Adair looked up to see an Apache about a hundred yards off on a rock outcropping, cradling a rifle in his arms.

Shortly after they'd noticed the sentry, the mesquite and cotton-woods soon changed to piñons and scattered scrub oaks causing MacLaren to note that they'd probably climbed to over four thousand feet. Though the horses were not moving on, they were struggling against the grade and the thinner air. MacLaren was just about to insist that they stop to rest when the narrow trail broke out on a scenic mesa which was alive with Victorio's renegades. Women and children were at work cooking, putting the finishing touches on their wickiups and tending to the other endless details of living as the men sat by and watched.

It was only a moment before everyone took note of their intrusion. Warriors grabbed their weapons and began jabbering and shouting to one another, as they surrounded Cain and the two white men.

MacLaren recognized a dozen of the men, including Ciervo Blanco, one Apache he'd like to have seen dead.

The camp was alive with tension. MacLaren looked around. To his left he saw Nana limping toward the crowd which had already surrounded them. To his right he saw something that caused his heart to skip as instant anger and utter disgust collided in the pit of his stomach. Bile roiled up in his throat almost choking him.

"Jesus Christ Almighty, Jack," Adair groaned when he saw the same thing.

Two hundred feet to their right a trio of naked white men were hung up by their hands on tripods, only the balls of their feet touching the ground. All MacLaren saw at first was the bloody chest on the man to the left and a head of blond hair on the slumped-over head of the middle man. All were sunburned the color of red chili peppers.

"Good Christ, Jack!" Adair added as though they were his dying words. "Kriss."

"I see it, Harley," MacLaren said, working hard on his composure. "Just hold your britches on and try to take no notice of it."

"Jack MacLaren!" Nana shouted as he limped through the crowd, sounding like he was greeting a friend who'd just stopped by to say hello.

Before MacLaren could answer, he looked down to see Ciervo Blanco stroking the walnut stock and the long brass scope on his Remington Creedmore. He fought the impulse to kick the Apache's teeth out. Instead, he quickly dismounted, landing between his horse and Ciervo Blanco. "You ought to keep your hands to yourself White Deer," MacLaren said quietly just as Nana appeared in front of his horse. Seeing the tension, Nana shot a back-off look to Ciervo Blanco.

"What brings you to our camp in these troubled times, Jack MacLaren?" Nana asked, as Adair and Cain dismounted under the scrutiny of fifty pairs of hostile eyes.

"I have important business with your father," MacLaren said. "I must talk with him right away."

"If you bring us another peace offering from the bluecoats, you can keep it for yourself. We will hear of no more treaties from the men with forked tongues in Washington," Nana said directly and with passion, his friendly tone quickly turning businesslike. "Those times are passed."

"I know they are," MacLaren said to the son of his Apache friend. "And it pains me to know that," he added quietly.

For a long moment everyone was silent as MacLaren locked eyes with Nana.

"Come. I will take you to my father's lodge," Nana said, breaking the somber silence. "He will be pleased to see you."

MacLaren slowly reached up and slid his stubby twelve from its saddle sheath as if it was the natural a thing to do.

"You stay," Nana said to Adair as he and MacLaren walked off.

The crowd began to relax and dissipate slowly, children resuming their play, men and women going about their business. A half dozen warriors stood with Cain and Harley Adair. Adair was mesmerized by the sight of the tortured white men.

"Your friend will be safe, Jack MacLaren," the Apache said as he hobbled off, showing the way.

The route to Victorio's wickiup went right in front of the three tall tripods. By the time they were abreast of the captives an Apache woman had picked up a hardwood switch and was beating the prisoners on their backs and asses, all the while laughing with two other squaws. The women were obviously moved to resume their torture by MacLaren's presence. The switching was getting only a random groan from the white men. And none of them raised their slumped heads.

150

As he went by, MacLaren recognized the other two. Kriss Andersen was bracketed by Jason McClintock on the right and Ernie Eldridge to the left. For some odd reason, MacLaren could only think that it was a happy day for the Governor of Texas. The Apaches had peeled Eldridge, front and back. If he wasn't dead already, the man known far and wide as the man who busted the Governor's jaw was only hours from it. "God damned politicians always get the last laugh," MacLaren mumbled under his breath.

The heavy Apache woman was switching Kriss with moderate blows. She seemed more like a woman lazily beating a carpet. All she could get from the kid was an occasional grunt. MacLaren noted that they'd cut on him some, but he was still alive. McClintock was still in one piece but probably closer to the grave than to the world of the living.

Nana limped toward his father's lodge as though the torture tripods and their grotesque captives didn't even exist. MacLaren understood the Apache. A prisoner being tortured to death got little more notice than a squaw weaving a basket or a kid skinning a rabbit.

MacLaren turned his head back as he followed Nana past the captives. Kriss raised his head after one of the blows and looked directly at MacLaren. But his eyes were blank. There wasn't a hint of recognition in the boy's face.

When he saw Kriss Andersen's eyes he knew what he had to do.

31

MacLaren followed Nana to Victorio's lodge. The wickiup was a crude affair fashioned from curved saplings covered with animal skins which looked like they'd been thrown in place at random. Shaped like half a pumpkin, the lodge had a doorway which caused MacLaren to hump over as he passed through.

"Sit, Jack MacLaren," was all Victorio said. It wasn't a friendly greeting.

MacLaren lowered himself on to the skins which covered the floor.

"I am sad that we do not meet at another time," Victorio finally said. "These are bad times for the Apache. The bluecoats want to make squaws of us and move us to far away places where there is sickness and no game. Your white brothers pushed us to far."

MacLaren looked at the chief. He lifted his dusty, black, flat-brim Stetson, combed his fingers through his hair once and reseated the hat.

After a short pause, he spoke. "Those people are not my brothers," MacLaren said, letting Victorio know he didn't appreciate the Chief making the connection. He paused again and glanced briefly at Nana who had taken a seat to the left of his father. "Victorio, you and I have talked often and agreed that there could be room in the Territories for all men."

"The room they make for us is San Carlos, or the Florida swamps," Victorio said, his regal face glowing with anger through the long black hair which flowed down over the front his shoulders. "This we will not accept."

MacLaren had the impulse to offer to try to arrange talks between the Army and the Chief, but he knew it would be a useless suggestion.

"I can see your thoughts, Jack MacLaren. You must keep them to yourself. We have taken a journey which follows only one trail and we know where the trail will take us," the Chief said, the initial tension in his voice evaporating to a certain sad, sonorous timber. "There is no turning back." Victorio paused and lowered his eyes. "No turning back on anything," he said, letting MacLaren know that there was nothing he could do to accommodate Jack MacLaren.

Just as Victorio finished his sentence, there was a loud visceral groan from one of the prisoners hung up fifty feet from Victorio's lodge. The animal noise was as close to a scream as the victim could muster. Whatever the Apache women had done, it struck them funny and the laughter from the squaws continued.

MacLaren winced at the noise and came alive with a sense of urgency. "I've got to ask a favor, my friend," MacLaren said directly to Victorio, ignoring the Chief's admonition that he could not help MacLaren. Again he glanced momentarily at Nana. "That boy you've got hung up out there is a special friend to me. He is like a son to me," MacLaren said, surprising himself with the intensity of his admission. He paused to collect himself. "I want you to give him to me. I don't want him harmed any more."

Victorio saw the pain on MacLaren's weathered face. But he answered MacLaren bluntly. "This can never be," he said. The white hair you called a boy has killed many Apaches. He rode with the white devil, McClintock. He is now the property of Ciervo Blanco, his squaws, and his little brother, Mano Suerte. Mano Suerte watched the white hair kill his father, Lanza Roto. You know of Ciervo Blanco. He would never give the boy to you. Ciervo Blanco was born with much anger in his heart. And you know an Apache chief can only ask for something, never order it. Apaches are a free people. We are not ruled by a government like the white man."

"The boy also has anger in his heart," MacLaren blurted out. "Your warriors killed the boy's mother, father, and two little sisters up near Mineral Hill after you killed the Buffalo Soldiers at Fort Sumner and started your war with the army."

"All are angry," Victorio said. "We must avenge the deaths of many Apaches."

"Father," Nana opened cautiously. "I will talk with Ciervo Blanco. Jack MacLaren is our friend. I live only because Jack MacLaren saved my life when most white men would have shot me like a horse with a bad leg and sold my hair to the white government. I will try to help him with the white hair he calls a son."

MacLaren turned to Nana. "If the boy is set free, you and your people have my word that I will kill the boy myself if I have certain knowledge that he ever again kills an Apache for vengeance."

Victorio nodded approval of the oath to Nana. The Chief knew MacLaren's promise was not a ploy.

"I will tell this to Ciervo Blanco," Nana said as he got up to leave the lodge.

"Nana," MacLaren said, looking up at the Apache, who paused to listen. "The boy has killed the Apache. The Apache has killed the boy's whole family. This is sad, an injustice to everyone. If we continue to trade in this vengeance it will go on 'til the end of time. This is foolishness and it troubles my heart. But if the boy is killed you also have my word that I will avenge his death."

"Talk if you wish, my son," Victorio said to Nana as he waived him on his way. "But you talk to a man possessed by bad powers, a man who will not hear your words."

Nana left Victorio and MacLaren in silence. It was unsettling because the two men had always had so much to say in the past.

"You and your friend must leave at once," Victorio finally said to his friend. "There is much hatred here for the white man. You know that I have no power over my people except the power of my deeds and power of my words. In these times I grow weak among my people. The Apache is free to make his own way. You know these things. Most have decided that there is honor in death, and that there is no honor in living under the rules of the white man. Since they have chosen death, no words from their Chief can change that. The coming of the white man has made my people look toward the next world where game is plenty, where the land is owned by all men, a world where there is no white men." The chief paused, and then added quietly. "This is sad. It is sad because I do not think there is another world. There is only this world and nothing beyond."

MacLaren somehow felt that what was happening at that very moment was a crazy dream. He felt like he was looking in from the outside, an observer, not a participant. The kid was hung up outside half dead. His old friend Victorio was speaking of his end. He and Harley Adair were in the midst of a hundred warriors who would love to see two more tripods with two more naked white men hung up. He knew Nana had only one chance in a thousand of getting Kriss Andersen set free. And there he sat, worn down from a lack of sleep with his .12 gauge cradled in his lap, two buckshot loads in the chambers and six in the leather shell holder laced around the stock.

He'd acted impulsively when he set out to find the kid. It was his way. And his instincts rarely let him down. In the war, he'd learned to always move forward, reacting to events as they unfolded. But as he sat there in Victorio's crude lodge, he realized that his impulsive three day ride across New Mexico and Old Mexico and to the Sierra Del Piñitos was likely to come to a dead end. No matter what the end, he had decided that he wasn't going to leave Kriss Andersen to be tortured to death.

"Like the Apache, I believe that there are things worse than death," MacLaren said quietly, his eyes lowered to the shotgun in his lap.

Victorio grunted, making a sound which indicated that he understood.

The next thought to traverse MacLaren's mind caused him to smile. He was thinking about how surprised Joe Harper would be when he found out he'd inherited the Sable Laire and how angry Mary Beth would be to lose him to the Apaches.

"Victorio," MacLaren said when his scattered thoughts collided with Harley Adair. "The man who came with me has no part in this. He has never drawn Apache blood. He is a friend and a lawman. Governor Wallace ordered him to arrest McClintock but he arrived too late. Send him away safely."

"I will ask for his safe passage as I will ask for yours," Victorio said just as Nana ducked into the wickiup.

He didn't need to say anything. Nana's eyes told the story.

MacLaren got up and faced the son of the great Chief. "You are a good friend, Nana," he said clamping his left hand over the Indian's right shoulder, his .12 gauge dangling from his right hand.

Victorio got up and retrieved the Winchester carbine leaning against the side of the lodge.

"Jack MacLaren! I ask that you respect my wishes and go from here. The White Hair's fate is decided. When you and your friend have gone, I will make sure the boy suffers no more," Victorio said. "It is all I can do."

MacLaren didn't answer. He turned, pushed aside the deerskin flap, and ducked out of the lodge into the morning sun. The Chief and Nana followed closely. The camp became suddenly still. Every Apache looked toward their Chief, their brown faces filled with hatred for the white man. Harley Adair searched MacLaren's face for instructions but saw nothing.

MacLaren walked slowly toward the three tripods. Two squaws stood behind McClintock, bloody skinning knives in their hands. Kriss was out cold, but MacLaren couldn't see any killing wound on the boy. The primordial noise he'd heard must have come from McClintock. They'd pealed half his back and a bloody rectangular flap of skin hung grotesquely. The squaws were smiling a stupid smile. MacLaren's eyes were on fire.

"You red bastards can take this body," Jason McClintock growled, his gravely voice coming straight from Hell. "But my spirit will live in many white men until the last Apache is dead."

Several of the Apaches who spoke English gasped. The noise McClintock made didn't seem human.

In one fluid motion, MacLaren drew his knife and slashed the braided rawhide rope which held the kid up. The kid fell to the ground in a heap. Cain and another warrior grabbed Adair's arms as he instinctively went for his Colt. Several others led by Ciervo Blanco and a skinny kid at his side, moved in on MacLaren. MacLaren leveled his .12 gauge on Ciervo Blanco's gut and calmly returned his knife to it's sheath.

Several of the Indians looked pleased with the potential for a confrontation between MacLaren and Ciervo Blanco. MacLaren thought he saw several wagers in progress.

"White Deer, you killed this boy's mother, father, and sisters. I am told that the White Hair killed your father. For that I am sorry," MacLaren said as the group moving on him stopped. "It is my hope that the killing can stop. This boy is my friend. He is like a son to me. If the killing can stop, I will take him home with me. If that can not be, there must be more dying. And it will start with you," MacLaren insisted, his eyes revealing the truth in his words.

"You got my answer from Nana, MacLaren. The White Hair is mine. He belongs to me and Mano Suerte and my wives," Ciervo Blanco growled. "We have no war with you and your friend," he added, pointing toward Adair. "You may go. But the White Hair is mine."

"No man belongs to another man," MacLaren said, taking two steps toward the Apache, his mind racing, his .12 gauge still pointed at the Indian's gut. "I'm leaving with the boy."

An eerie quiet fell over the camp as the two men faced off. MacLaren would let the Apache say the next word and break the silence.

"No!" the Apache shouted, spittle shooting from his mouth. "The boy is mine," he said loudly, speaking to others in the camp as well as to MacLaren.

MacLaren took note of the fact that no one jumped in on Ciervo Blanco's side. The Apaches knew that Ciervo Blanco had refused a request made by both their Chief and Nana, a respected warrior in his own right. And he figured Victorio and Nana for the kind of leaders who rarely asked for favors.

156

"I'm leaving with the boy," MacLaren said, taking his chances. "Unless you feel you can stop me. Or do you need your squaws to help you," He added impulsively.

The Apache went off like a cannon, dancing around and screaming in an odd mix of his native tongue, Spanish and English.

MacLaren got the gist of Ciervo Blanco's explosive harangue.

"He says he will fight you with knives," Nana said. "Whoever lives takes the boy."

Except for the scrap where he'd gutted Burleigh Simmons, MacLaren hadn't been in a knife fight in a dozen years, and then it was with a drunken drifter he was trying to lock up. But it gave Kriss a chance. He was about to accept the challenge when Victorio stepped between them and firmly and politely asked Ciervo Blanco to let the boy go. "Again, I ask this favor for my friend, Jack MacLaren."

Just when it looked like Ciervo Blanco might give in, McClintock let loose with a string of blood curdling oaths aimed at the Apaches, insulting everything they held sacred. An Apache stepped up and shut McClintock down with a rifle butt to the temple.

Ciervo Blanco took a step toward the Chief and growled, "No. I will kill this white man you call friend."

"Victorio," MacLaren said from behind. "We will fight to settle this. That is fair," MacLaren added. "But I must have your word that my friend, Harley Adair, goes free, no matter the outcome."

"You have my word," the Chief said, stepping back, suddenly looking tired and older than his years. "The man who harms your friend will answer to me."

MacLaren handed his shotgun to Victorio, slid his knife from its sheath and took a step toward Ciervo Blanco. "White Deer," he snarled. "You're no warrior. You are a killer. You kill for fun, not for your people. I have felt pain for every man I have killed in battle," MacLaren went on, trying to anger the Apache. "But killing you will cause me no pain. You have bad spirits in your head. Your powers are evil powers," MacLaren said as he began to circle to his left, his knife held low. "The spirits will never let you go to the next world. You will never have peace, White Deer."

Ciervo Blanco's eyes were glowing white hot. The veins in his neck were purple and throbbing with uncontrolled anger.

Just as the Apache was about to lunge at MacLaren, Nana stepped between them, his own knife drawn. "There will be no fight," Nana said. "I say the boy goes with Jack MacLaren," he said looking around at his fellow Apache's. "Jack MacLaren came here to ask friends for help. We must not disgrace ourselves just to allow Ciervo

Blanco to satisfy his thirst for blood. This white hair means nothing to us."

"Nana," stand back, MacLaren said. "This is my fight."

Victorio stepped up, his Winchester at the end of his outstretched arm, a fence between MacLaren and his son's back. "Nana has spoken," he said quietly. "Move back, Jack MacLaren."

Ciervo Blanco was momentarily taken aback by the intrusion of his fellow warrior. Every Apache respected Nana as a fearless warrior and an honorable man. Ciervo understood the challenge and faltered, but then in a flash of madness he lunged at Nana slashing as he went. Nana was slow to move and Ciervo Blanco's knife cut a shallow wound in his left forearm.

Nana looked down at the blood dripping from the cut and then looked up at Ciervo Blanco with a smile. "You are a fool, Ciervo Blanco," Nana said as he began to circle his adversary, his pronounced limp giving him an odd look. "Jack MacLaren is right. You would harm your own brother like a child pulling the wings off a bug," Nana continued, taunting the crazy Apache. "You ask many favors of your Apache brothers, but you offer none. Now you must fight me, your equal in battle. I will not fight like a squaw or a white man."

Unable to hear another word, Ciervo Blanco charged Nana, his knife high over his head, his body boiling with raw anger.

Nana saw his opening. He sidestepped the mad charge, grabbed his foes right wrist, and drove his own knife deep into Ciervo Blanco's gut. Nana held the wrist in an iron grip and lifted up on his knife, tearing through Ciervo Blanco's innards, literally bringing the Apache off the ground as he worked his knife around in Ciervo Blanco's chest. The dying Apache kicked madly but Nana held his deadly grip, his muscular arms bulging. Suddenly Ciervo Blanco opened his mouth, vomited a stream of purple blood, and went limp. Nana angrily threw the dead Apache off his knife and looked around to see if any others wanted to fight for the white hair.

32

"Go at once," Victorio said to MacLaren as he handed back the cut-down shotgun. The Chief's face was a mask of frustration and anger. "Take the boy with you. And do not return to our camp."

Then the Chief turned toward Cain and the others who had surrounded Adair and the four horses. Victorio waived them off with a nod of his head.

MacLaren went at once to Kriss Andersen, cut the rawhide ties on the kid's swollen, bloody wrists and ankles, and rolled him on his back.

Kriss opened his eyes briefly and then they rolled back in his head.

"Harley, get me pants and a shirt from my saddle bags. And a canteen!"

The Chief said something in his native tongue and the crowd slowly disbursed. People went about their business as two squaws fell to their knees next to Ciervo Blanco and began wailing over his body. The young Mano Suerte stood aside, staring dumbly at the bloody remains of his older brother.

MacLaren noticed several groups of men jabbering and looking his way, obviously not pleased with the way things had gone.

Adair came forward with the four horses, rifled MacLaren's saddle bags and came up with pants and a shirt.

"Get him covered up," MacLaren ordered as he got up and went to his horse, all the while keeping his shotgun ready in his right hand. "We have to get the hell out of here before some of White Deer's hothead friends decide to pick up where he left off."

While Adair struggled to put the clothes on the kid's limp, sunburned body, MacLaren found the small tin container he was looking for. He opened it and dropped a pinch of salt into the canteen and shook it. He knelt next to Kriss and poured a small bit of the briny water into the kid's mouth. Kriss choked the water down but didn't return to his senses.

As MacLaren got up, his eyes locked up with Jason McClintock. "Help me," McClintock groaned. "Don't let 'em have their way with me." McClintock's words took MacLaren aback and brought a lump of pity to his throat. MacLaren imagined that it was the first time in his life Jason McClintock had ever asked a favor of another human being.

"Go, MacLaren!" Victorio insisted again, his impatience reaching its limits. "You can not help these men."

MacLaren turned away.

Jason McClintock hoped he'd gotten his wish. He thought he'd caught MacLaren's nod as he turned away.

"Mount up, Harley," MacLaren ordered. "Behind your saddle. I'll hoist the boy up. He'll ride in front of you."

Adair climbed into his saddle and then scooted back. His horse fidgeted and danced. MacLaren, now sweating profusely from his hurried effort, lifted the limp kid up, and he and Adair wrestled Kriss into the saddle.

MacLaren then retrieved the canteen of salty water and handed it up to Adair. "Make him drink a sip every fifteen minutes or so."

MacLaren turned and walked toward Victorio and Nana. Nana was wrapping his cut arm with a strip of blue calico. MacLaren offered his hand and Victorio took it and held it firmly. "Until we meet again, Victorio," MacLaren said.

Victorio said it all with his eyes. They would never meet again.

"Chief, stop the raids in the Territories. Spend the winter with your people hunting and fishing. The white chiefs in Washington will not send the Army here. They are tired of the fight with the Apache. One day they will ask for peace. You could have many good summers to enjoy Nana's children and their children."

"Go, Jack MacLaren," was all Victorio could say. MacLaren had his answer.

MacLaren touched the brim of his dusty hat, and turned to Nana. "Take care of your father, my friend."

"I will," he answered. "Now you must leave. There are many here who wish you harm."

MacLaren turned away from his friends, sheathed his shotgun, and quickly mounted his tired gelding. He maneuvered his horse to face Victorio and Nana. "You have my word that the location of your camp will not be revealed. And if you ever need my help, come to the Sable Laire. You will always be safe there."

Victorio allowed a thin smile and raised his Winchester above his head.

"Let's go, Harley," MacLaren said as he nudged his horse forward.

This final picture of Victorio was burned into MacLaren's mind. As he rode out of the Indian camp, a wave of distress crashed over his body and then quickly receded. Hell, he thought to himself, the Chief doesn't need my pity! Victorio will die a free man. He's lived as one with forces of nature, including the most devastating force of all, the dark side of man. He's known the pleasures and sorrows of the flesh and the spirit. In life he's had everything worth having, and known all that was worth knowing. In death he will find honor, and pure freedom. In death he will escape the humiliation of watching his people destroyed and enslaved by the white man.

* * * *

The two men rode as hard as they could considering the circumstances. For the first half hour they saw Apache lookouts observing their progress and then, finally, the sentries were gone. Though his mind seemed dead, Kriss Andersen's body had revived to the point where he was able to hold on to the saddle horn. Nonetheless, Adair had to hold Kriss upright with his left arm as he managed the reins with his right hand.

Finally, certain he was beyond Apache eyes, MacLaren pulled up. "Give the kid more water," MacLaren ordered, his demeanor still tense.

Adair tipped the canteen up into the kid's mouth and Kriss choked the salty water down.

"Kriss!" MacLaren said loudly and he examined the kid.

"Jack?" Kriss mumbled, his head still slumped.

MacLaren tried to talk to the kid but he got no intelligible responses. Several of his wounds were leaking through the red calico shirt and his sun-blistered face had a gray pallor.

"Harley, the kid doesn't look good. You go on. I've got unfinished business here," MacLaren ordered, acting like a military commander. "You've got to get the kid to a doctor."

"Jack, I guess I know what you've got in mind," Adair pleaded. "It's a damn fool notion. I say it ain't worth the risk."

"I can't leave those men there like that," MacLaren said directly.

"Hell, those boys drew their cards and made their bets, Jack," Adair said frankly. "Leave it be. You'll never get those men out!"

"You ride on with Kriss and the spare horses. Stay east on this trail until you're out of the foothills. Go northeast and you'll soon run into the Los Gatos Wash. Ride that big wash north. If you hold a steady pace, you'll be in the Arizona Territory two hours after you hit the wash," MacLaren commanded. "There are small towns on the way. Find a doctor for the kid. If you can't get help and Kriss isn't coming around, ride on to Fort Bowie. I figure there's a U.S. Army doctor there. I'll try to catch up. Keep moving and change horses. If the kid comes to his senses, put him in your saddle and you go bareback on one of the other horses."

"Jack, I don't think...." Adair started to say. But before he could finish, MacLaren had reined his horse around and charged off. "You damn fool!" Adair shouted after him.

MacLaren raised his right hand as he galloped away, his way of letting Adair know that he was probably right.

MacLaren retraced his steps for a half hour, and then left the trail and began picking his way carefully toward a high rock formation he'd noticed on the way out. He hoped it would provide a panoramic view of the area, including the mesa where Victorio was camped.

When it was soon obvious that his horse could climb no further, he tied his reins carefully to a small juniper tree and hobbled the tired gelding. After loosening the girth on his saddle, he dumped the last of the oats he had into his canvas feed bag and strapped it to Gunn's bridle. He'd pushed Gunn hard since Monday morning and he would soon be pushing the horse even harder.

His horse settled, he got a box of his custom made .45-70 cartridges from his saddle bags and pulled his Remington Creedmore from it's sheath. His juices began to stir as he started his climb on foot with the eleven pound rifle resting on his shoulder.

After a ten minute climb, he reached the perch he'd picked out earlier. It was better than he'd imagined. The mesa scattered with Apache lodges was right before him, but there was a good five miles of winding trail from their camp to where he'd left Gunn. It would give him a slim lead.

MacLaren picked a spot behind a fallen, rotting juniper tree. He rested the rifle on the downed tree trunk and began surveying the area below through the thirty-three-inch-long 4 × 15 brass telescope on the Creedmore. He could see most of the camp clearly. As the crosshairs passed by the three tripods, he saw that Ernie Eldridge was still hanging by his hands and appeared lifeless. But the Apaches had

162

hung Jason McClintock upside down and tied his hands tightly to his thighs. They were stoking a small fire under his head. Every three of four seconds, McClintock would jackknife to keep his head from the fire. The event had drawn a big audience and MacLaren could see that the Apaches were getting a big kick out of McClintock's performance.

MacLaren cocked the single shot rifle and then thumbed back the rolling block. He fingered one of the special target cartridges from the box at his side, slid it into the chamber, and thumbed the block forward.

He took a moment to guess the distance again and judge the wind. There was only a slight breeze from the west. "Five hundred yards," he mumbled to himself.

Centering the telescope cross hairs high on his target, he took a deep breath and began to exhale slowly. Just as his lungs were about empty, he squeezed the trigger. The large rifle bucked and settled back on the rotting log. Its muzzle blast echoed across the canyon. MacLaren quickly focused the scope on his target again just in time to see the slug smash into Jason McClintock's chest, sending the dead man swinging like the pendulum in a grandfather clock. The Apaches didn't know what was happening until they heard the blast of the .45-70 rifle arrive a couple of seconds after the slug.

MacLaren watched the Apaches scatter and then took another look at McClintock. He had a hole the size of a man's fist high in his back. The Indians would have no more fun with Jason McClintock.

MacLaren methodically ejected his spent brass, and slid a fresh cartridge in the chamber of the Remington. Though the former Texas Ranger looked dead, he fired at Eldridge. The shot was wide to the left and sent more Apaches running for cover as the large slug cut a furrow in the red soil beyond the tripods. MacLaren reloaded. The third shot hit the Ranger dead center.

His business finished, he rolled on to his back and momentarily rested the rifle in his lap. He threw his hat aside and massaged his face and scalp with both of his weathered hands. For a moment, he wondered if McClintock and Eldridge weren't one up on him now. For them the struggle was over. But his thoughts quickly turned to the living. Kriss, Harley, Mary Beth, Joe Harper and the boys. He snatched up his hat and scrambled to his feet. It suddenly struck him that he faced a long run on a tired horse. Before he turned away, he saw warriors going for their horses. There'd be a bunch of angry Apaches who wouldn't take kindly to being cheated out of their fun.

MacLaren's stumbling retreat down the rocky path took only a couple of minutes with gravity on his side. When he made his way to his horse, he shoved the big rifle into its scabbard, stowed the shells, untied the feed bag and threw it aside. In one fluid motion, he undid the leather hobble, cinched his saddle, and mounted Gunn.

The big horse sensed the tension and jigged and danced down the rocky path to the main trail. On the main trail, MacLaren turned toward Arizona and kicked Gunn into a steady extended trot.

*   *   *   *

In the Apache camp, several of the followers of the dead Ciervo Blanco scrambled for their weapons and ponies. The skinny Mano Suerte ran in circles shouting oaths of revenge. Victorio walked to the center of the camp and fired his Winchester in the air. The frenzied activity ceased as the Apaches all turned toward their respected chief.

"This is finished," Victorio shouted as he pointed his rifle toward the upside down body of Jason McClintock. "We must not risk our people here by riding off for vengeance. We must not act in anger."

A few of the mounted warriors argued, but it was obvious that their passions were under control.

"We must move from here. We must leave at once for Tres Castillos. We will winter there," Victorio insisted. "No Mexican soldier or white man will bother us there."

Epilog

Jack MacLaren leaned on a new fence post and sipped a bottle of beer he'd just pulled from the chilly springtime waters of the Rio Largo. It had been another fine day under clear skies. He and his six hands had strung a quarter mile of fencing on the southern border of the Sable Laire. It was a breezy afternoon and the land was alive with dancing wild flowers and waves of lush green grasses. It had been a harsh winter and that made spring all the better.

But the recent weeks had been marred by the news of Tres Castillos. Two weeks earlier, hundreds of Mexican soldiers, allied with a large number of Tarahumara Indians, had cornered Victorio and his people at their camp at Tres Castillos. The soldiers and the Tarahumaras had swept down on the sleeping Apaches after saturating the camp with rifle and cannon fire.

Though details were still sketchy, the papers had claimed that the two-day-long, pitched battle had ensued because railroad financier, Jefferson Burns, had told President Díaz that further investments in Mexican railroads were conditional on Díaz killing Victorio and his warriors. The papers also claimed that a half-breed Apache the Mexicans called El Machetazo had sold Burns the location of the Apache camp for one thousand dollars in gold.

Harley Adair had been reinstated as a U.S. Marshal on the order of Judge Beck the day after he rode into Fort Bowie with the half-dead kid.

Two weeks past, Adair had told MacLaren that he'd had certain knowledge that Cain had traded Victorio for gold.

As he took another swallow of the cool beer, MacLaren wondered again, as he had done a hundred times since he'd heard the news, how and why men like Cain come to be.

Newspaper accounts of the battle claimed that the Apaches not killed in the initial assault had been backed up the steep canyon wall and had to be routed out one by one in hand to hand combat.

When it was all over, seventy-eight Apaches and one hundred and fifty-five of the attackers lay dead. One of the dead was Victorio, the great Mimbres Apache Chieftain. The papers had reported that the Mexican commander had paraded his body through dozens of villages while the Mexicans committed untold acts of desecration on the body of the Chief. There were differing reports on how the Chief died. Several Mexican soldiers took credit for his demise, but MacLaren's preferred the likely story that Victorio had taken his own life with the last cartridge in his Winchester when his capture had been imminent.

Curiously, there was no word of the killing or capture of Nana. MacLaren assumed that he'd escaped the battle. Remembering the ferocity of Nana's deadly encounter with Ciervo Blanco, MacLaren reasoned that Nana would probably give the white man fits for years to come, especially when he heard the stories of the desecration of the body of his father. And Geronimo had taken up the hatchet when he'd heard of the slaughter of Victorio. The Apache wars weren't over yet.

All the events of the year past had taken their toll on Jack MacLaren's sensibilities. From where he stood, the world was going to hell. At times he laughed at himself and wrote it off to the approach of his fiftieth year, and he often chuckled out loud as he caught himself saying the kinds of things his father had said during the late fifties as the Civil War approached.

But as he leaned on the fence post, he reasoned that it wasn't just age setting in. He figured, man was on a journey that had a beginning and an end. As the cold brew mellowed his mind, he imagined how New Mexico must have been before the Spanish conquerors and the tidal wave of white Americans from the East. The idea of life as the Apaches had lived it in the centuries before, appealed to Jack MacLaren. Living off the land. No governments. No merchants or banks. No railroads. No fences!

He often wished he'd lived in those times. And he often dreaded the future. He was certain man would multiply his number, invent bigger and better machines, and try to overcome the forces of nature. Governments would grow to protect the weak of mind and spirit. Nations would make wars that would dwarf the war between the North and the South. The weak would inherit the earth for a time. And then Mother Nature would step in and sweep man away. God would write off his experiment with man as a total failure.

Jack MacLaren was certain that the ways of the Apache would produce eternal harmony in nature while the ways of the white man would breed chaos.

MacLaren was awakened from his beer-soaked philosophizing by footsteps from behind.

"Supper's ready, Jack," Joe Harper said as he approached. "You know better 'n to keep old Cass waitin' once he's got grub ready."

"Oh, Howdy Joe," MacLaren said as he took his weight off the new post. "You know, Joe, this land must have been something before all the people....all this civilization."

"Good Lord, Jack! It still is somethin'," Harper said. "Ain't any people but the six of us for miles around. Now come on, quit your fool daydreamin'. Let's eat before someone else gets to our grub."

MacLaren swallowed the rest of his beer and walked quietly back to the camp on the Rio Largo.

The others were already tearing into thick venison steaks which had been wrapped in bacon and cooked slowly over mesquite coals. The black beans and rice, heavily laced with onion and garlic, and the fresh-baked molasses bread stirred MacLaren's stomach juices.

"You boys already done frigged yourselves out of the best cuts of meat," old Cass Dixon mumbled through his wild beard as he worked furiously on a chunk of the tender venison with his new false teeth. "Better sit and grab what's left before that's gone too!"

MacLaren laughed out loud at the sight of the old timer he'd taken in years back. Cass Dixon had been a swamper in a Las Vegas sa-. loon. He used to sweep up for whiskey. Just after he'd staked out the Sable Laire, he'd found Cass in the street one night. He'd thrown him over his horse and hauled him to the ranch. He'd been there ever since, sober as a judge all the while.

As far as MacLaren was concerned, Cass Dixon had earned his wages forever and hereafter for his campfire humor alone, never mind his skills as a farrier and chuckwagon cook.

MacLaren and Joe Harper grabbed tin plates and scooped beans and rice from the big cast iron pot which sat at the edge of the cookfire grate which crowned a circle of neatly placed stones.

"Grab a piece of that meat, Jack. It nearly melts in your mouth," Kriss Andersen commanded. "And old Cass has worked wonders on that brown bread."

MacLaren smiled at the boy, drew his knife, leaned over and stabbed at one of the thick steaks on the grate. The kid had been slow coming back to the world of the living, but his body had repaired well over the winter. MacLaren still wasn't certain about his mind.

Kriss had explained that the last thing he remembered before waking up at Fort Bowie, two weeks after Harley had brought him in, was the squaws peeling Jason McClintock's back. He'd remembered kicking out at one of the squaws carving on McClintock. The next thing he'd remembered was being hit in the head with a war club by the skinny little Apache he'd let go during the Hatchet Valley ambush.

"Damn, Cass! You've done it again," Joe Harper said as he took his first bite of venison.

While the men ate, they talked about fences, cows, women, guns, horses, and anything else that came to mind.

After supper, MacLaren went to the river and pulled five more bottles of beer out of the cold springtime water. He passed beer around to all but Cass who poured a cup of fresh coffee. He sat back down on the folding camp stool, and held his bottle up. "I want to make a toast, boys. This is a special day."

The men looked at each other with blank faces, obviously unaware of reason to celebrate.

"One year ago this very day I found 'White Hair' here shot twice and mostly dead," MacLaren said looking directly at Kriss Andersen, the lad who'd been tagged "White Hair" by those who knew him.

Kriss looked up, his memory restored. MacLaren saw that the anniversary had, in fact, escaped the kid's mind.

"The sorry part was that his people were some of the first to die in the Victorio War," MacLaren said quietly. "The good part is that Kriss kept the Devil from gettin' a hold of me before my scheduled time. Me and Harley Adair, both! The lucky part was Kriss drawing a Grand Jury that wouldn't hand down murder indictments against him and Bowles."

The men chuckled softly and Kriss looked down at his bottle.

"I know you boys will all agree when I tell you that no young man with only seventeen winters to his credit has ever been so shot, cut up, and beat up and still come out of it with his head on straight and his sense of humor still in one piece."

"Ain't that so," Joe Harper sighed.

"So here's to you, Kriss," MacLaren said. "There'll not be an April 4th that will ever pass that I don't ponder my good luck."

Kriss still had his head ducked, his big Stetson hiding his trembling face and his moist eyes.

"And whatever you do, Kriss!" MacLaren said loudly. "Don't let that sense of humor run out on you. It becomes more important as the years pass you by!"

Joe Harper stood up and the other four followed. "To 'White Hair'," Harper said as he turned his bottle up. The men quickly finished their beer and went to the river for another.

"What the hell happened in Janos anyway?" Cass Dixon asked Kriss, Cass had stoked the fire and the others had settled in around the flickering fire. "Tell us the story."

Kriss Andersen, paused, pushed his Montana Peak Stetson back on his head, and then started with their departure from Elmira, New York. "Well," he started. "It all came to be because my Mother's damn fool relations drove my Father crazy. They said he wasn't a Christian man. He listened to it for years, and then one day...."

For some years to come the story of a kid they called White Hair graced many a campfire in the Old West.

But as the years passed, the names Jack MacLaren and Kriss Andersen vanished from the local folk lore. Only the name Victorio lived on as men imagined an earlier time when a free man like the Apache Chief could ride as one with the wind.

Coming Soon
From
Fanjoy & Bell, Ltd.

The Copper Queen

by Ed Hewson

Mail Order Form

Fanjoy & Bell, Ltd.
P.O. Box 5035
Manchester, NH 03108-5035
1-800-984-9798

Please send me _____ copies of:

Apache Sundown, by Ed Hewson

ISBN: 0-9652112-0-7

1 Copy @ U.S. $10.00
2 to 5 Copies @ U.S. $9.00 per copy
6 to 10 Copies @ U.S. $8.00 per copy
Add U.S. $1.00 shipping and postage for one copy.
Add U.S. $0.50/book for orders of more than one book.

I am enclosing a check in the amount of $_____ .

Name: _____

Address: _____

_____

City/State/ZIP: _____